MOORLAND FARM

An enchanting and unforgettable historical family saga

GWEN KIRKWOOD

Sinclair Family Saga Book 2

JOFFE BOOKS

Revised edition 2023
Joffe Books, London
www.joffebooks.com

First published by Robert Hale Ltd.
in Great Britain in 2016

This paperback edition was first published
in Great Britain in 2023

Cover art by Jarmila Takač

ISBN: 978-1-80405-852-7

In memory of the late Dorothy Lumley
who was my agent for thirteen years and was always
encouraging and cared deeply for my interests.

Also with fond memories of my late grandson
Christopher who so loved his books.

Thank you to my granddaughter Sarah for her
technical help with this novel.

CHAPTER ONE

William Sinclair stood in the doorway of the cowshed at Moorend Farm, his spirits sinking as he watched the estate's land agent cantering towards him. Only one thing could be bringing Mr Rowbottom back so soon. Lord Hanley owned the land and as landlord, he had every right to refuse his request for an extension to the lease on the farm tenancy of Moorend. William's lean jaw clenched. Ten years ago he and Emma, newly married and with a baby son, had left their native Scotland under a cloud of disapproval. Ever since he had been determined to prove they would make a success, both of their marriage and their enforced move to Yorkshire, and they would do it without the help and influence of his family. He swore he would never go running back to Bonnybrae like a prodigal son.

Farming was a long-term business. It took time to build up good relations with a new landlord, and it needed a lot of hard work to get land back to fertility when it had been as badly neglected as Moorend had been when he took on the tenancy in July 1897. He shuddered as he remembered their arrival. He and Emma had only been married the day before, although Jamie was already six weeks old. That was their secret and they had kept it to themselves. They were strangers in the small Yorkshire community of Silverbeck and they had no intention of creating gossip for the locals. They had resolved to make the best of a new life together as man and wife, hopefully leaving their past and its prejudices behind them.

They had worked hard to make a decent home and eke out a living with only a Clydesdale mare, two cows and a few hens, plus the feeding sheep they had taken on each year as temporary grazers to make the most of their share in the common land. All but two small paddocks of Moorend Farm had been left fallow, or rank with overgrown grass. It had taken long hours of toil behind the horses, ploughing, sowing, reaping and mowing, only to start all over again the following spring as year followed year. William had thoroughly cultivated each of the fields in turn, bringing them into rotation and gradually building up fertility.

His strategy had enabled them to keep more cows and so produce enough milk to sell to the town and bring in an income. He didn't know what more he could have done to prove himself a worthy tenant so he would be bitterly disappointed if Lord Hanley could not give him credit for his hard work and his success in restoring the land to productivity. They were happy in their marriage too, with five healthy children. They were not wealthy, but they paid their rent on time, they were making a living and had no debts. They were both strict about that. Emma was thrifty and she worked hard to keep a clean home and a good table. There were no cottages attached to Moorend Farm so they needed to provide board and lodgings for their workers. Emma understood men needed to be well fed if they were expected to do a good day's work and both men and maids liked and respected her.

All William wanted now was a guarantee that he and his young sons would still be tenants here to reap the benefits of their toil in years to come. It didn't occur to him that any of his sons might refuse to follow in his footsteps, so he wanted to ensure the future for all of them at Moorend. William knew his capacity for work, his organisation, and his knowledge of land and livestock had earned the respect of Lord Hanley's land agent. In fact, they had come as close to being friends as their positions were likely to permit, given Bob Rowbottom's responsibility for the whole estate and his authority to negotiate with the tenants. He had seemed in favour of extending the lease when they discussed it and it was well known that Lord Hanley valued his opinions and usually acted on them, so William's frustration was all the more intense.

'Why are you looking so glum this fine spring morning, William?' Rowbottom asked cheerfully as he drew his horse to a halt. 'Perhaps this will cheer you up.' He drew a letter from his leather pouch. William took the envelope warily. The paper was thick and of the finest quality, the writing neat and beautifully executed, even better than Emmie's and she was good, especially considering her only education had been at Locheagle village school, back home in Scotland.

'I was hoping for news about the lease but this doesn't look like a business letter, judging by the hand writing.'

'It isn't. Lady Hanley addressed the envelopes herself. Aren't you going to open it, man? I'm sure your wife will be pleased. She deserves an evening out more than any wife I know. Lord and Lady Hanley are giving a dinner up at the manor house. It's not a regular occasion but this is for those tenants who usually pay their rent on time. The women will be vying with each other for the most fashionable dresses — but I vow you'll have the prettiest woman there.'

'I see,' William said slowly, but without enthusiasm.

'It's an honour, man! As a matter of fact Lord Hanley is keen to meet Mrs Sinclair. He knows all the wives of his other tenants because most of them are local and married neighbouring farmers.'

'Why should he be keen to meet my wife? He's an old man. Well, maybe not that old, but he is compared to Emmie.'

'That doesn't stop him, or any other red blooded man, admiring a pretty woman.' Bob Rowbottom chuckled at William's indignant expression. 'He knows she has given you three sons, and recently a second daughter. He thinks you're aiming to supply him with tenants for all fifty-two of his farms.'

'It is true Emma and I find it all too easy to have babies,' William admitted with a rueful smile, relaxing a little. 'But even we can't produce fifty-two children. Does he consider me a good enough tenant to consider my sons for a tenancy when they are old enough? That's what I want to know. Where I come from it is nearly always the father's influence, and his reputation as a good farmer, which secures the tenancies.'

'Aye, it's often the same down here.' Rowbottom's expression sobered. 'Between ourselves I think he's waiting to meet your wife before he makes a decision about increasing the length of the lease for Moorend.'

'Surely a farm lease depends on the tenant? Though I must admit I don't know what I'd do without Emma. We're a good partnership.'

'A good wife is more important to a man's happiness, and his success, than we give her credit for, if you ask me. I know Lord Hanley would agree. He has heard that Mrs Sinclair helps you with the milking. Not many of the farmers' wives in this area do that these days, especially if they have a brood of youngsters.'

'Polly helps with the bairns. She's been a maid with us since we first came to Yorkshire. She was only fourteen and newly left the school.'

'Aye, I know. She's a niece of Joe Wright, the blacksmith. He was telling me how much she enjoys working at Moorend. I hear her brother is working for you as well now.'

'He is. Tom was a skinny young laddie when he came as a temporary helper but he has proved reliable and honest, like his sister. He has an instinct with animals and enjoys working with them. That's a bonus when we have a herd of dairy cows to tend seven days a week. I wouldn't like to lose him now.'

'You still have Cliff Barnes? Not many men would have had the patience to supervise poor old Cliff.'

'He can't help the brains being battered out of him when he was a youngster and he works hard and never complains, at least not so long as he gets plenty to eat.'

'That's a lot of extra cooking and washing for your wife.'

'It is, but we don't have much option if we want an income from milking cows. Milking twice a day, seven days a week takes a lot of labour and Moorend doesn't have any cottages for a married man or we would have preferred that.'

'Only a few of the farms on the estate have workers' cottages, but most of them are in the village, or near enough for their workers to live there. None of the other tenants keep as many cows as you do, so they don't need as many men.'

'I know, but we're doing what we do best. Since wee John was born Emma has employed a woman from the village to help with the washing and ironing and do some of the cleaning. The blacksmith's wife, Ivy Wright, recommended her. She's a widow called Maisie Blackford.'

'I'm sure she'll be good if Ivy recommended her,' Rowbottom grinned. 'Joe and Ivy know everybody around Silverbeck, and their pedigrees.'

'Well she's right about Maisie. Emma says she's a treasure and she gets on well with Polly. She works three days a week and seems happy to come. Apart from needing the money, she says it's a pleasure being where there's children and sharing her meals with us. I suspect she gets a bit lonely with no family of her own. When she's here it means Emmie is free to help with the milking so that pleases both of us. She says it lets her have a seat on her milking stool and a break from the children. Emmie doesn't consider milking the hardship some people think.' He smiled. 'She milks with me and Tom most afternoons. Polly prefers to feed the young calves.' William smiled proudly. 'Our wee Meg was nine in June so she likes to help with the young animals.' He frowned. 'Jamie is the eldest though so it's time he learned to milk, but he would rather be in the fields with the horses and machines, or rounding up the sheep on the common with his dogs. I must admit he is good with them. He often talks with the gypsies when they're camping on the common for the summer.'

'Maybe he senses you prefer to have your women folk around you,' Bob Rowbottom grinned. 'I'll report to Lord Hanley. He wondered how you were managing since we made so many extra stalls in the cowshed for you, but he agrees it was a good idea to extend right through into the bullock shed since you seem to have your mind set on dairy farming.'

'It was Emma's idea to use the bullock shed once she had seen that the loft above ran the length of both sheds.'

'Mmm, she has more than a pretty face then. She must be in favour of you keeping the extra cows too. Lord Hanley thought he might have wasted his capital if you couldn't manage thirty.'

'It's a lot of work but so far the income has been regular and reliable, although we did hear one of the buyers from Leeds has gone bankrupt. The farmers who supplied him lost two months' income. It's a risk we have to take because dairying and sheep are what I've been used to all my life.'

'And none of the other tenants have a wife who helps as much as yours, eh?' Bob Rowbottom grinned. 'When she meets the wives of the other tenants at Lord Hanley's dinner they'll be telling her she is spoiling you.'

Emma was both nervous and excited when she heard about the dinner.

'Go to Wakefield and buy yourself a new dress,' William said, smiling at her excitement. 'You deserve one. Bob Rowbottom would agree.'

'I don't need a new dress.' She looked up at him with the dimpling smile that could still make his heart skip a beat. 'I shall be able to get into my wedding dress. Marie is only two months old so I'm a normal size for once. It's the most lovely material I'm likely to find.' William knew his sister Maggie had helped her choose the material back home in Scotland. They had made their dresses together for the wedding. He sighed. He still missed the company of his elder brother, Jim, and his sister Maggie. He was glad Emma was a good letter writer. Maggie always replied promptly giving them all the news of Bonnybrae and his family. She visited Emma's parents too and he knew Emma found that a great comfort.

'I remember how lovely you looked at our wedding, Emmie, but all the other wives will be getting new dresses. Fashions change, don't they?'

'Yes, but I shall take out some of the material. Maggie and I gathered it to the back according to the paper pattern. That was the fashion ten years ago. I will shorten it a bit to show my ankles.' Emma's eyes sparkled with mischief as she lifted her skirts a little.

'You do tempt a man, Emmie,' William said, his voice deepening. 'You have trim ankles on your lovely legs. I've noticed them, you know,' he grinned, raising his eyebrows in the way which brought the colour to her fair skin. She knew the only time he saw her legs was when they were in bed. 'Seriously, Emmie, I would like you to treat yourself to something special.'

'We-ell . . . I would like to have a pair of fine leather shoes instead of wearing my Sunday boots. I have enough money from selling my eggs and butter to buy them. Apart from that it might be a chilly wind at the end of March for the journey home in the pony and trap. I might make myself a warm cloak. I wish I knew how to make a proper coat with sleeves and a collar — I ought to be able to make one now you've bought me a treadle sewing machine. The seams are much faster and stronger than sewing by hand.' She sighed. 'I'll buy some woollen material and some satin for a lining. A new cloak will do fine and we'll take a rug for our knees for coming home.'

'I know you'll look lovely, Emmie. Mr Rowbottom thinks so too. It's a good job he's nearly old enough to be your father, and with a wife and grown up family or I'd be jealous.' William was inclined to be a possessive husband. Emma had grown into a very attractive woman, with a passion and spirit to match his own. Neither of them had expected such satisfaction from their marriage when circumstances had thrown them together.

Emma had never been able to keep her slim figure for long with having five babies in ten years so she was looking forward to dressing up for this occasion. She sensed it was important to William that she should look her best and she prayed she would not let him down. She was skilled with her needle so she enjoyed remodelling the blue-green brocade she had worn for her wedding. It matched her eyes and emphasised her fair skin. She could wear her ring with the three little diamonds too. William had said it was supposed to be an engagement ring but they had never had an engagement. He had bought it five years after they were married. No one in Yorkshire knew the circumstances of their marriage. It was their secret. William had a half-cousin named Drew Kerr living in Yorkshire so he and his wife, Annie, were the only ones who knew of the strife surrounding their marriage and the misery they had both suffered. A plain gold wedding ring had been sufficient then. There had been no money to spare for luxuries. Then shortly before John was born, William had arrived home triumphantly with the diamond ring in a small leather box.

'One of the breweries bought our Clydesdale gelding,' he announced jubilantly. 'I always knew Peggy was a good mare and would prove to be a good breeder, even though everybody down here thought she was too small compared to the Shires. I got a better price than I expected. The manager of the brewery asked if I had any more horses to sell that I had broken myself.' Emma knew he was proud of the little Clydesdale mare he had earned by sheer hard work when he first came to Yorkshire. 'I promised myself I would buy you a diamond ring as soon as we could afford any wee extras. I'm sorry it has taken me so long.' Even now the tears sprang to her eyes when she remembered William's boyish pleasure at being able to present her with the ring. Her own joy was that he had even thought of such a thing because she knew well enough there was always something required either for the farm or for the children and household. Whenever she looked at the ring she wondered what his mother would have thought. Mary Sinclair was proud and haughty and she had never forgiven William for dallying with her maid and marrying beneath him. She never wrote. His father James and eldest brother Jim often sent messages through Maggie's letters. Emma's first daughter was called Meg but she had been christened Margaret Eliza after

Maggie and her own mother. William was still too bitter to name their second little girl Mary after his mother. They had compromised by naming her Marie Emma.

Bit by bit Emma had made Moorend a home to be proud of and she loved her children dearly, but secretly she longed for her parents to be able to visit. Although her mother wrote every week, Emma's one regret was that they and her three brothers had never seen her children or where she lived — she had not seen them since her marriage.

As the evening for the tenants' dinner drew nearer Emma grew increasingly nervous, wondering how she would manage to talk to so many strangers. She had asked William to stay by her side but he had told her that after the meal the women would withdraw with Lady Hanley while the men each went in turn into Lord Hanley's study to pay their rent.

Emma had become well acquainted with Miss Grace Hill who owned the haberdashery shop in Wakefield. She had gone there since her very first visit to the city and over the years she had bought all manner of materials and wools for knitting socks for William and the children and making clothes for them. She took a small piece of material from her dress and explained about the dinner and that she wanted to make a warm cloak for the journey home. Miss Hill showed her various swathes. Emma sighed.

'I wish I knew how to make a proper coat with sleeves.'

'Oh my dear,' Miss Hill exclaimed, 'you must call on my sister-in-law. She trained as a tailoress in Leeds before she married my brother. Since he died she has set up in a small shop doing alterations to earn a living. She may not be able to make a coat in time for the dinner but she could advise you.' She explained where to find the little shop down one of the side streets. 'We often recommend each other.'

So Emma found Mrs Hill and immediately felt at ease with the plump little woman with her cheery smile. She looked about ten years older than her sister-in-law.

'I do have several orders to fill,' she said anxiously, 'and I don't like letting people down when I've fixed a date for a garment to be ready, but I don't like turning away a customer either. I know you are a loyal customer to my sister-in-law. She told me you keep her supplied with butter and fresh eggs.'

'Yes, that's right,' Emma smiled. 'Oh well, I shall make do with sewing myself a new cloak instead, though a coat would have been more serviceable for going to the kirk — er . . . to church I mean.'

'A cloak?' Mrs Hill's face brightened. 'I may have just the thing you could borrow to wear to Lord Hanley's dinner. I made it for my daughter to wear over her wedding dress because she was married in the winter and it was a fair walk to the church. Will you wait while I run upstairs to my living quarters? If you don't like it there's no harm done, but if it would be suitable I could make you a good warm coat later on.'

She returned with a black velvet cloak with a hood. It was lined with pale blue satin. 'My daughter is about the same height as you,' she said as she placed the cloak around Emma's shoulders. 'Velvet is not very practical for every day so Sarah has never worn it again, but I think it would be suitable for evening wear. What do you think, Mrs Sinclair?'

'I think it's lovely, and much more — er, more elegant than a woollen one I would make myself.' She dimpled a smile at the older woman. 'If you're sure you don't mind me wearing it. I would like a coat to wear to church for next winter.'

'In that case I shall wrap it in a parcel. Would you like me to take your measurements to save you coming back? Then I can tell Grace how much material we need for the coat and the lining and you can pay both of us when it is finished, or pay Grace for the material when you're next in town.'

'That will be splendid, if you're sure Miss Hill will not mind?'

'She knows you're honest and reliable my dear, so don't worry.' She busied herself wrapping the cloak into a neat parcel and added some black lace gloves.

Emma was delighted with her outfit. She demonstrated the velvet cloak the following morning.

'Oh Mrs Sinclair, you do look lovely!' Polly clapped her hands together.

'You'll be the prettiest woman there,' William said with a pleased grin. 'Now I'd better get off to market. I'm meeting Cousin Drew at the cattle ring today.'

When he came home later that day Emma guessed he and Drew Kerr must have been for a drink of whisky, or two. He was in high spirits as he changed his clothes ready for the milking. She was surprised when he presented her with a narrow black leather box. When she opened it she thought it was a bracelet made of triple gold links side by side, then she saw it was actually a dainty gold watch on an expanding gold bracelet. It had a black dial with greenish numerals.

'It's beautiful, William,' she breathed softly, scarcely able to believe her eyes. 'Can we afford something so lovely?'

'You're worth it, Emmie.' He grinned down at her. Neither of them were extravagant and William didn't often buy gifts, but when he did it was always special. He seemed to derive a boyish pleasure in giving them to her. 'Try it on. It is supposed to be luminous so you can see it in the dark. Shall we go into the cupboard under the stairs to try it?' he whispered, giving her a roguish grin. They both knew it was more than a look at the watch he had in mind. She punched him playfully on his broad chest but she reached up to kiss his lips.

'We cannot linger anywhere right now, William Sinclair,' she chided softly. 'Polly and Mrs Blackford are waiting in the kitchen and the cows are tied in the cowshed waiting for us to start milking. You'll have to wait until tonight,' she added in a whisper, her eyes sparkling like a summer sea. She couldn't resist holding out her wrist to have one more look. 'It really is lovely, William. See how the bracelet gleams. It will be very useful too when I go shopping and need to catch the train home. I'm always searching for a clock in the shops or on one of the churches.'

'I'm pleased you like it, Emmie. Promise me you'll not be nervous at Lord Hanley's dinner. Remember you're as good as any of the women there, however high and mighty some of them consider themselves.'

'At least I shall know our neighbours. Evelyn Tindall is always friendly. She did say one or two of the tenants' wives think they're a bit above the rest of us, though.'

William knew she found it impossible to forget she had once been a maid at Bonnybrae. He silently cursed his mother's condescending manner and the way she had cast Emma out. She had proved herself the best of wives. He had grown to love her sweet modesty and their past was no one else's business.

CHAPTER TWO

They started the milking earlier than usual the following afternoon and Emma left the byre promptly to make sure she had plenty of time to wash herself and give baby Marie a good feed at her breast, although she knew Polly would give her a top-up from a bottle if she was hungry. They had both learned a lot about rearing children since the day they arrived at Moorend, with Jamie a young and fretful baby.

Emma knew William loved to see her with her long dark hair loose, falling in waves down her back and over her breasts. He always ran his fingers through her silky tresses but Emma felt she could not wear it that way to go to a dinner party. She kept it in neat pleats pinned into a thick coil during the day when she was working but she didn't want anything so severe either. Maggie had helped her pin it on top of her head the day she was married and even her brother Joe had admired it and said it made her seem taller. Maisie Blackford had agreed to stay the night to help Polly with the children. She would sleep in Meg's room, with the boys in the room next door so she would be sure to hear if any of them got up in the night before Emma returned.

'Can either of you help me pin my hair on top of my head?' Emma asked, appearing in the kitchen in her white underskirt with a shawl around her shoulders. She had tried several times to pin the heavy tresses in place and she was frustrated.

'Oh Mrs Sinclair, you have beautiful hair,' Mrs Blackford exclaimed. 'I have never seen it loose before. If you sit on this chair I could try to coil it on top of your head. I used to do my sister's, and she did mine, when we were going somewhere special.' She smiled and blushed. 'I might need you to help me Polly, because it's a long time since we did such things.'

Between them, the two women pinned Emma's hair in shiny fat curls on top of her head, showing off her slender neck. 'Your hair has a natural curl. Do you think we should have a little ringlet down each side, Polly?'

'Yes, I think so,' Polly agreed eagerly. 'It would soften the effect and we can always pin them back up again if you don't like it. Meg, will you run upstairs and bring down your mam's mirror from her dressing table so she can tell us what she thinks?' None of them had heard William enter the kitchen. He stood in silence for a moment. Emma had often surprised him with yet another facet of her personality.

'You look a perfect lady, Emma.' He beamed at Polly and Mrs Blackford. 'I could recommend you both as ladies' maids to Lady Hanley.'

'You can't do that,' Emma said. 'We couldn't manage without them.'

'I should have bought you a necklace instead of a watch, now I see you like this.'

'Oh no, William. I much prefer my watch.' She extended her arm for Polly and Mrs Blackford to admire her husband's gift. 'And it will be far more useful too. I could wear the pearls my mother sent me for my twenty-first birthday. If you think they'll be suitable?' she added diffidently. William knew she meant were they good enough? His face softened.

'They will be perfect. Come upstairs and I'll fasten them on and help you put your dress over your head. You may need to help me fasten my collar and cufflinks.'

Emma sensed this dinner was important to William and she hoped she would not let him down. She had come a long way from the innocent young girl who had gone to work for his parents at Bonnybrae but she knew she still had a lot to learn about the wider world and how men and women behaved. Neither of them had been inside the manor house before, but Mr Rowbottom was standing beside Lord Hanley waiting to greet them as they entered. Both men seemed to know the tenants and their wives already which made Emma even more nervous, although no one would have guessed as she held her head high and looked every inch a lady in her velvet cloak and brocade gown. Mr Rowbottom smiled and said her name. She guessed this was for Lord Hanley's benefit. He held out a hand to take hers, then unexpectedly clasped his other over the top.

'A small hand, but a very capable one, I hear,' Lord Hanley said with a smile. 'I am pleased to meet you at last, Mrs Sinclair.' Emma met his eyes and saw only kindness there, although she knew he was reputed to be a shrewd judge of character as well as business. William had told her he had two sons who were in their thirties but he looked older than she had expected. The party of tenants and their wives numbered roughly forty . The ladies were directed to a room to leave their coats and cloaks before being shown straight into a long dining room by a stern looking man, whom Emma assumed must be the butler. She looked around with interest and saw there were two marble fireplaces, which seemed strange until she noticed the room had a partition in the middle, folded back against the wall. She supposed it divided the long dining hall into two separate rooms when there were fewer people. Several young men asked their names and guided them to their seats. Each place had a gold-edged card to indicate its occupant. Lady Hanley was already standing at the far end of the long table keeping an eye on proceedings. Emma felt a pang of dismay when William was led away from her to sit on the opposite side of the table. He smiled across reassuringly as soon as he reached his place on the other side. They were only about four seats from the end where she presumed Lord Hanley would be seated, but she was glad they were not at the end nearest Lady Hanley. She was relieved when Mr Tindall was seated next to her and his wife, Evelyn, next to William on the other side of the table. At least she was acquainted with them and they had both chattered freely on the few occasions they had met.

'Lord Hanley must have had a good year when he's giving a dinner like this, for all us lot, eh lass?' Tindall boomed jovially.

When they were all seated, the young men came round with wine for the ladies and beer or cider for the men. Lord Hanley gave a brief welcome speech then the meal proceeded. Emma was glad she knew which cutlery to use as she watched Mr Tindall fumbling with his. He leaned closer and asked, in as low a voice as he seemed able to manage, 'Which of these bloody spoons and forks am I supposed to use? And what's this little bugger for?' He lifted the small tea knife in disgust.

'That's right, Emma, you keep him right, lass, and tell him to mind his language,' Evelyn Tindall called across the table with a wide smile. Conversation flowed as the meal progressed. The woman on Bill Tindall's other side nudged him and indicated the man on her left.

'Gerry Wilkins wants you to introduce him to Mrs Sinclair. He's been asking me who her husband is and why he's seated nearer the top of the table than he is.' She spoke in a low voice but Emma heard her above the hum of conversation and wondered whether there was supposed to be an order of precedence amongst the tenants. She glanced across the table, realizing the haughty looking woman diagonally opposite must be Mrs Wilkins. What a sour face she has, Emma thought.

'Aah, so you're the couple from Scotland who came down here to show us Yorkshiremen how to farm, eh?' Mr Wilkins said in a tone that hovered between jovial and irritable. 'I've heard about you from Mr Rowbottom, Mrs Sinclair. He tells me you can milk the cows as well as the men and you make the best butter in the district. I wish my wife milked the cows for me,' he added with a half-laugh. His wife glared across at him and then at Emma. She drew her chest up like an angry hen, fluffing out its feathers.

'If you wanted a dairymaid, Wilkins, you should have married one. I was never so desperate for a man I needed to be his skivvy.' Her voice was sharp and carried clearly in the sudden hush of conversation. Emma raised her dark, well-marked eyebrows in mild surprise. A smile curved her lips as she looked across at William but he seemed tense and anxious. She bit back her smile but her eyes still danced with laughter at the woman's foolish outburst. It was a blessing she didn't know all their history. Her opinion of her as a dairymaid was of no consequence, as Emma found the milking both satisfying and relaxing, and she was happy to work beside a man who loved her. She saw William relax. He smiled warmly back at her and her heart gave a familiar skip at that certain look in his eyes. As she glanced away she was surprised to catch Lord Hanley's gaze on them. Her eyes widened when he gave an unmistakeable wink. A whimsical smile spread across his face before he bent his head to speak to Mrs Rowbottom who was seated on his left, although her husband was at the other end of the table next to Lady Hanley. Mrs Rowbottom glanced at Emma and nodded in response to Lord Hanley. Across the table Mrs Wilkins gave a haughty sniff when everyone seemed to ignore her and continued with their conversations.

'I reckon her Ladyship's annoyed because you and your husband are nearer the head of the table than she is,' Mr Tindall said in the nearest he could get to a whisper. Mrs Wilkins glowered angrily at him and then at Emma. 'The Wilkins are the biggest tenants on Lord Hanley's estate,' Mr Tindall went on. 'It doesn't make a bit of difference to Gerry but she never lets anyone forget it if she has an audience. She'll be jealous as hell now you're milking more cows at Moorend than they are at Mountcliffe. I heard the railway porter remarking that Moorend was sending more cans of milk to the creamery than any of the others.'

'Surely nobody could be jealous about that,' Emma said. 'Looking after dairy cows is what William does best and it's what we're both used to doing. I expect the other farms keep sheep or grow more crops than we do.'

'Mrs Sinclair!' Mrs Wilkins claimed Emma's attention in a peremptory tone. 'I was speaking to you. I hear you have Maisie Blackford working for you. I asked her to come to work for me but she says you keep her busy at Moorend. I want her to come to me Mondays, Wednesdays and Fridays. Now you know I need her, I'm sure you can rearrange your work and tell her you can manage without her for two of the days she works for you. I have a woman to do the cooking and some cleaning but I shall need Mrs Blackford for cleaning and laundry work.' For a moment Emma stared in astonishment at the woman's assumption that she could arrange other people's lives.

'Maisie has never mentioned wanting to work anywhere else,' she said, but her heart sank at the prospect of her leaving Moorend. She was a treasure and she got on well with everybody. 'I don't own her. She is free to work where she wishes, but we would miss her if she leaves. Apart from her work, she mothers Cliff Barnes.'

'Cliff Barnes? Isn't he the half-wit fellow? Do you still have him working for you?' She screwed up her face in disgust.

'Cliff is not a half-wit!' Emma said sharply. 'He is honest and kind and a very hard worker. It is true he needs a lot of supervision but he has no family of his own and he responds to Maisie's kindness.'

'Whatever you say,' Mrs Wilkins sniffed, 'but I am expecting you to tell her she is free to work three days a week for me. I need her to start in a fortnight. My daughter is going away on a world tour and I shall miss her.' Mrs Wilkins had raised her voice, making sure those around her would hear.

Emma saw William's anger as he opened his mouth to speak but Lord Hanley drawled, 'What's all this about a world tour, Gerry Wilkins? I can't afford to send my sons travelling in Europe, let alone around the world. I shall need to have a word with Mr Rowbottom. We can't be charging you enough rent.' Mr Wilkins glared at his wife and spluttered angrily. Emma had a strange feeling that Lord Hanley was not serious about raising the rent but he seemed to enjoy provoking the Wilkins.

'You've got it all wrong, your Lordship,' Wilkins protested. 'Thora's exaggerating. Our Irene is only going to France.'

'And Germany, and Switzerland,' Mrs Wilkins corrected. 'Maybe even Italy . . .'

'You told me it was only France,' he said accusingly. 'Anyway our lass is going as a maid to Major Turner's widow,' Mr Wilkins insisted, turning to Lord Hanley. 'She's getting old and frail so she wants a strong young lass to help with her luggage and look after her, make arrangements and sort out problems with hotels and her food. Our Irene's not used to earning her keep, as I keep telling her. I reckon she'll be glad to get back home.'

'She is not going as a maid!' his wife denied furiously. 'She will be a companion. It's a wonderful opportunity.'

'I hope it will be as wonderful as you seem to think,' another man remarked. 'My brother-in-law is Jewish. He lives in Leeds but he has relations in Germany. He reckons there's trouble starting there and worse is brewing, even though the Socialists didn't win this time in the Reichstag elections.

'It must be safe,' Mrs Wilkins insisted sullenly. 'King Edward and Queen Alexandra visited France in February.'

'I haven't heard of much trouble in France,' the man responded. 'It's at its worst in Russia, and I hear it's spreading in Germany. Anyway, the King would have plenty of guards.'

Lord Hanley stood up and pushed back his chair, bringing the conversation to an end. He thanked them all for coming and said the men would remain behind to finish their drinks and come through to the estate office in turn to pay their rents. The ladies would accompany Lady Hanley upstairs to the withdrawing room.

William immediately took Mrs Tindall's arm and escorted her around the table to Emma's side. His wife smiled gratefully at him. He knew how nervous she had been at the prospect of him leaving her on her own but he was making sure she had Evelyn Tindall for company.

'Avoid that battleaxe Mrs Wilkins, if you can,' he whispered. 'Don't stand any trouble from her.'

'Good evening, Mr Sinclair.' A smiling, middle-aged woman joined them. 'I'm Bob Rowbottom's wife, Janet.' Her eyes danced as she greeted them and Emma had a feeling she had overheard William's whispered comments. 'Lord Hanley has asked me to accompany these two ladies. I already know Mrs Tindall, but he asked me to introduce your wife to some of the other women.'

'I'm pleased to meet you, Mrs Rowbottom.' William gave her his most charming smile.

'Mmm, you are a handsome lad, and no mistake, when you smile like that. I can see why you agreed to marry him and move to Yorkshire.' She smiled at Emma. 'I wouldn't like to cross you, though, William Sinclair. I saw the way you scowled when Mrs Wilkins was making her demands. I was relieved when Lord Hanley intervened before you could speak your mind, not that I could blame you, but she would never forgive you.'

'She thinks she's two steps up from Lady Hanley herself does that one,' Evelyn Tindall said bluntly.

'Then we must shield Emma from any more encounters with her sharp tongue. Your wife will be quite safe with us, Mr Sinclair. I know you are our youngest tenants but my husband seems very impressed with the way you have reclaimed most of the neglected land at Moorend. He tells me you get along well with the gypsies too. He used to have a lot of trouble with them tearing down fences for firewood, and grazing their animals on other people's land, but he says you seem to know how to handle them.' William was saved from replying when Bob Rowbottom came to have a quick word with his wife. He greeted Evelyn Tindall and Emma before moving away to join Lord Hanley in the estate office.

'Oh — I nearly forgot.' He came close to them again. 'Lady Hanley asked if you will introduce Mrs Sinclair to her, Janet. We couldn't hear the conversation down your end of the table but we felt waves of tension coming our way. Presumably that was due to Mrs Wilkins?'

'I'm afraid it was. Lord Hanley didn't like her arrogant manner and she was implying that her daughter was going on a world tour. He already knew Major Turner's widow had hired the girl as her general dogsbody for her trip to Europe. You know how quick he is to put people in their place when he thinks they're too big for their boots, but I'm afraid it was poor Gerry who suffered from his humour. I'll bet Mrs Wilkins hears about it when they get home. Also, she wants to steal Mrs Sinclair's maid while Irene is gallivanting.'

'What! You can't allow that, Emma. You need Mrs Blackford far more than Mrs Wilkins does. She gets on well with you, doesn't she?'

'Yes,' Emma sighed. 'We have a happy household, even if it is a busy one. I don't want to lose Maisie Blackford but I can't keep her against her will.'

'I don't think she would choose to go to Mrs Wilkins, not if she knows you have work for her. You should ask her about it tomorrow and make sure she knows you need her. We all like to be needed.'

'Thank you, I will. I was wondering whether I should mention it to her.'

'I don't think you need to worry. Maids never stay long at Mountcliffe and Mrs Blackford will know that. Gerry is such a genial fellow — I don't know how he puts up with a wife like that.'

'I reckon you know very well how he manages.' Evelyn Tindall gave him a dig in the ribs. 'You hear more gossip than any of us, even if you don't pass it on.'

'Do I?' Bob Rowbottom said, feigning innocence.

'Aye y'do. I'll bet you've heard the rumours that Mrs Wilkins has only let him into her bedroom once a month since that lassie was born. Irene must be twenty now. No wonder his horse is tethered outside Miss Cody's cottage for hours at a time, or so I've heard.'

'Miss Cody's?' Emma's eyes widened. 'Wasn't her father a vicar?'

'He was.' Evelyn chuckled wickedly. 'I expect that makes the sport even better for Gerry Wilkins. But she's also a very nice person,' she added seriously. 'He would have been a damned sight happier with her for a wife.'

'Come, come now, Evelyn Tindall, you will be having Emma believe we're a bunch of Yorkshire sinners,' Bob Rowbottom chided, but he was smiling.

'Oh, I don't think that,' Emma denied hastily. When he had gone to join Lord Hanley, she said to Evelyn Tindall, 'I did wonder how the Wilkins had only one daughter though. Poor Mrs Blackford would have loved to have children but she says they were never blessed with any, yet we find it almost too easy to make babies.'

'Aye,' Evelyn threw back her head and laughed, 'I can imagine that with a man like your William.' Emma blushed. 'But at least you know your husband is warming his own bed and not somebody else's,' Evelyn added more soberly.

'You are a one, Evelyn Tindall,' Mrs Rowbottom said shaking her head, but she was smiling. 'Come with me now and I will introduce Emma to Lady Hanley. I think she wants to ask you about your butter. They make butter at Manor Farm but she says yours is much better, when she is lucky enough to get it from Mr Nicholson's grocery shop.'

Lady Hanley was speaking to a group of tenants' wives, but she saw them approaching and stepped aside to speak to them. Janet Rowbottom performed the introductions then excused herself, saying she had drunk too much lemonade.

'Same here. I'll come with you,' Evelyn said.

'They will probably find a queue,' Lady Hanley said with a smile. 'I think most of the women have made an excuse to go if only to inspect the water closet Lord Hanley has recently installed. I expect a lot of them will be pestering Bob Rowbottom to get one for their houses when they discover an indoor water closet doesn't smell, as most of them thought it would.'

'I have never seen a water closet,' Emma said truthfully.

'Then you must go and take a look before you leave. Now Emma, tell me why your butter is so much better than the butter made at Manor Farm. Mr Nicholson tells me he can never get enough of yours.'

'He's been very kind ever since we first came to Moorend. He takes my eggs and any surplus butter to sell in his grocer's shop,' Emma said. 'I don't know why the butter should be any different though. The churn and all the wooden utensils must be kept very clean, of course. I scrub them with salt as soon as I have finished using them.'

'Your butter is so much sweeter and it keeps longer in the summer. Our own butter goes rancid quite quickly if the weather is warm. '

'The excess water will depend on churning the butter to a good grain, not over-churning into a fat ball. Then whoever works the butter with the Scotch hands will take out the excess before making it into moulds. The butter always keeps better if you have a good supply of clean, cold water. The gypsies say Moorend water comes from a spring high up on the common. It feeds the burn that runs at the bottom of the stack-yard. We're lucky to have a pump in the dairy to save us carrying water from the burn.'

'The burn? Ah — you mean the brook? I see. I suppose you don't have time to make enough to satisfy all Mr Nicholson's customers?'

'I enjoy making butter but it isn't only the time it takes which prevents me making more. After we skim off the cream to make it into butter, we're left with skimmed milk. I use some for cooking and we feed the surplus to the young calves, if we have any. Then there is the buttermilk to use after the butter forms into grains. It's excellent for baking the scones but I could never use it all if I was making butter every day. Some of my children like to drink it, and one of the men who lives with us. Sometimes the gypsy women come for some in exchange for their wares. Ivy Wright, the blacksmith's wife, says if we were nearer the village the women would be pleased to buy it, as well as the skimmed milk. As things are, we feed any surplus to the pigs but we earn more money if we take the cans of milk to the station and send it to the buyer in Leeds. So far we have been lucky because he has always paid up at the end of each month. We heard some farmers have been let down when their buyers couldn't pay, or have gone out of business. That would be a real worry. Our buyer carts it round the streets every day. William says the householders come out with their jugs to buy it while it's fresh.'

'Yes, I believe that is true. I had not considered what Lord Hanley would call the economics of the situation. Do you feel happy and settled here in Yorkshire, Emma, so far from your family?'

'I didn't want to move so far away at first,' Emma admitted honestly.

'And now?' Lady Hanley persisted.

'I sometimes wish my parents would come to visit and see our home and the children, but I know my mother will never make the journey. We exchange letters every week. I have told her all about the house at Moorend and I tell her about the children, so we keep in touch. When we first came, there was so much work to do with both the farm and the house being badly neglected that I didn't have time to be homesick and then . . .' She hesitated, remembering the fright she had had the first time she went to Wakefield and got hopelessly lost and pursued by a strange man, but it had all ended with William being so relieved to see her safely home he had seized her in his arms and told her how much he loved her. Her cheeks coloured at the memory. Meg had been born nine months later . . .

'And then . . . ?' Lady Hanley prompted, bringing Emma back to her surroundings. She looked up, her eyes still shining with her memories.

'Well, William loves me and we have our children, so home is wherever we are together. I know my husband is settled in Yorkshire now that he has got used to the different ways and accents. His cousin, Drew Kerr, lives a few miles away and they meet often at the market. Annie and the children are lovely and we visit each other sometimes. We are very fortunate, I think.'

'I am so pleased to hear you say so,' Lady Hanley said sincerely, almost with relief, Emma thought as Mrs Rowbottom rejoined them. Lady Hanley smiled at her. 'Emma and I have had a most interesting and satisfying discussion.'

As the evening wore on several of the tenants and their wives left when they had paid their rent, but there was no sign of William. Emma was glad of Mrs Rowbottom's company. She was pleasant and entertaining and she had introduced several of the other women. They all seemed friendly but Mrs Wilkins was hovering near Lady Hanley's end of the room, obviously wanting to talk with her. There were only six or seven men waiting to pay their rent when William came out of the office. He felt despondent. Lord Hanley had made no mention about the lease. Surely he must have made up his mind by now but he and his agent seemed in a hurry to deal with the remaining tenants. A lot of the young men who had served the meal seemed to have disappeared. Later Bob Rowbottom told him Lady Hanley had hired them, as well as extra maids for the kitchen, especially for the occasion. The Hanleys' own footman came to William with a tray and offered him another glass of whisky before making his way upstairs with a sealed note for Lady Hanley.

'I am to wait for your reply but his Lordship said a verbal yes or no would suffice,' the footman said as he handed the note to his mistress.

'Thank you, Thomas,' Lady Hanley replied. 'I think my answer will be yes, but I had better read this.'

William had already had two glasses of whisky and much as he liked his native tipple, he would not normally have taken a third glass while out visiting. He liked to keep a clear head for business, especially any meetings with Lord Hanley and his land agent. He drained the glass and set it down, then went to find Emma so they could take their leave. She had already expressed her gratitude to Lady Hanley for an enjoyable evening and a delicious meal, so as soon as she saw William she thanked Mrs Rowbottom for her company and hurried towards him. She noticed that Mrs Wilkins had got her way at last, but Lady Hanley seemed distracted and kept glancing round the room. Much to Mrs Wilkins' chagrin, she excused herself to say something to Mrs Rowbottom. She had seen Emma heading for the staircase to join her husband.

'Janet, could you detain Mr and Mrs Sinclair a little longer please? Tell them my husband would like a word before they leave.' Thora Wilkins opened and closed her mouth like a fish stranded on dry land. She fully expected Lady Hanley to turn back to her to finish her conversation. Instead, she was hurrying to the other end of the room to speak to the upstart Scottish woman again.

'She called them back,' she told her husband indignantly, 'and that woman had already spoken to her for ages. Some people are too ignorant to know when they should leave.'

'It seemed to me it was Lady Hanley who was detaining the Sinclairs, not the other way round,' Wilkins said. 'I wonder why?'

'He probably didn't pay all his rent. Lord Hanley will be wanting to know when he'll pay the rest before he lets them leave,' his wife surmised spitefully.

'Oh Thora, why do you always have to think the worst of folk? I reckon Sinclair can pay his rent as well as any of us now he's got the Moorend land into good heart. He's a damned good farmer and he works hard.'

'Oh aye, he works hard at having bairns, that's for sure,' his wife snapped. 'That's five they have now, I hear.' Her husband was silent. He had longed for a son to follow in his footsteps. Much as he loved his only daughter he was not blind to her faults and she had little interest in him, or the farm; only the money he could give her. He rather liked what he had seen of the Sinclairs tonight but he had long since learned it was not worth his energy to argue with Thora. She only saw one point of view and that was her own.

The rest of the guests had all departed when Lady Hanley led Emma, William and Janet Rowbottom into a small sitting room and asked the footman if he would bring a tray of coffee and biscuits and then tell the rest of the staff she would not require anything else tonight. Lord Hanley and Mr Rowbottom joined them shortly afterwards.

CHAPTER THREE

William wished he had not accepted that extra whisky. He began to wonder whether Lord Hanley instructed his footman to offer it to soften the blow when he refused his request for the extension to the tenancy agreement. He did not feel drunk. He had learned to hold his drink as a very young man back home in Scotland, but he knew he was not as clear-headed as he would have liked. He accepted a cup of strong coffee and refused the cream.

'Well, my dear,' Lord Hanley said, smiling at his wife, 'I suppose I must assume since we're all here that you agree with Bob's opinion?'

'Presumably you mean about extending the lease on the tenancy of Moorend Farm to give Mr and Mrs Sinclair more security?'

'That is exactly what I mean. Ten years is a long time. Anything could happen, to any of us.'

'But Mr and Mrs Sinclair are our youngest tenants and both you and Bob tell me you have been impressed by the way they have worked and succeeded in bringing Moorend back into full production.'

'That is true, but I was thinking more of my own advancing years than theirs.'

'Oh that's ridiculous. You're not that old and you've always been healthy. Anyway, we have two sons to carry on. Oliver will be home in eighteen months and I expect he will be eager to step into your shoes.'

'Humph, I'm not sure that's a comforting prospect.' He turned to look at William and Emma sitting side by side on a brocade settee. 'That is a very pretty dress you're wearing, Mrs Sinclair.' Lady Hanley's eyebrows rose. It was not like her husband to make personal remarks. He caught her glance and realized he had consumed more than his usual glass of brandy this evening. 'It seems you always win the ladies over to your side, William Sinclair.' He sipped his coffee.

'It is a very pretty dress. I thought so earlier,' Lady Hanley said, giving her husband time to drink his coffee and hopefully dilute the brandy. 'Did you buy it especially for this evening? I have not seen anything similar. Perhaps you sent to Leeds for it?'

'I-I'm afraid not,' Emma said flushing slightly. 'William thought I ought to buy a new dress for the occasion, but I love this material. I-I did alter the style a little at the back and I shortened the length.' She bit her lip. 'I'm sorry it is not quite the latest fashion.'

'Fashion!' Bob Rowbottom muttered. 'I doubt if even Lord Hanley knows what the latest fashion is for women. They're always changing. You look fine to me. I heard you admiring it earlier, Janet?'

'I was. I think it is lovely but I didn't know you had sewn it yourself, Emma.'

'I have always liked to sew,' Emma said simply. 'It is so much easier sewing for the children since William bought me a treadle sewing machine — and you can buy paper patterns for almost anything now from Miss Hill's haberdashery in Wakefield.'

'But I'm sure it still takes a lot of skill.' Lady Hanley smiled and turned to her husband. 'You see my dear, William Sinclair has chosen a wife who is both modest and skilled. I'm convinced she will be a great asset to him through the years.'

'Very well,' Lord Hanley drained his coffee cup. 'It seems they are all on your side, Sinclair. I will agree to extend your lease on Moorend to ten years. I shall have a new agreement drawn up, but it will be with one or two additional conditions. I want you to read it carefully before you sign it and if it is not to your liking, we shall renew the old lease and no ill felling either way. What do you say?'

'Say? I am delighted, Lord Hanley. I thank you. I had made up my mind you were going to refuse.'

'And if I had refused would you have settled down again quite happily?'

'I don't know. I would certainly have kept an ear open for any other farms coming to rent.' Emma's eyes widened at William's outspoken admission and she gave him a nudge, but he went on. 'I have three young sons growing up so I need some security for their futures too.' Later he admitted he would not have spoken so freely if he had not drunk so much whisky.

'Thank goodness Lord Hanley didn't seem to take offence,' Emma said fervently as she took the reins and drove the pony and trap home at a brisk pace.

Emma knew William was always more passionate when he had had a couple of drinks of whisky, as he sometimes did with Drew Kerr at the market, and this evening was no exception. Before she could pull her nightgown over her head he lifted her in his arms and rolled with her, skin to skin, onto the wide feather mattress. She sighed happily. It had been a lovely evening and William never failed to awaken her desire and carry them both to another planet, way beyond mere earthly pleasure.

The day before the year of 1908 began, Bob Rowbottom was just leaving Lord Hanley's office when he remembered the news he had heard while getting his horse shod at the blacksmith's.

'Mrs Sinclair had another baby boy yesterday. I hear they are both doing fine.'

'Another son, eh? Sinclair seems to know how to breed more than cows. That will be another farm he'll be looking to rent in the years to come,' he added drily. 'Give them my congratulations and good wishes if you're passing their way. Did you hear if Mrs Wilkins got her way over Mrs Blackford?' he asked curiously. 'I remember she was very arrogant over the matter at the rent dinner last spring.'

'Maisie Blackford didn't want to leave Moorend. I gather she said she wouldn't work for Mrs Wilkins even if the Sinclairs didn't need her. I think the Sinclairs are good to the folks who work for them, even if they are Scottish.'

'Does that make a difference?'

'I don't think it does now I know the Sinclairs, but Scotsmen have a reputation for being careful with their money. William is certainly shrewd and he doesn't suffer fools or cheats. Mrs Blackford stayed with them over Christmas so she would not be on her own, but I can't imagine anyone wanting to stay longer than needed with Mrs Wilkins. Apparently Maisie has no close family since her husband died. She had only been back in her own cottage a couple of nights when she was needed to stay at Moorend again because the baby was born. I heard this one had been a more difficult birth than the others.'

'It seems to me perhaps Moorend Farm should be the first of our tenants to get a water closet. It's certainly a busy household,' Lord Hanley mused.

Bob Rowbottom whistled. 'Poor old Wilkins. His wife will fly into a real rage if she hears we have improved Moorend farmhouse before Mountcliffe.'

'I'm sure you'll manage to smooth her ruffled feathers with your silken tongue, Bob,' Lord Hanley grinned, then he sobered. 'The Wilkins may rent the most acres but they have the smallest household. Wilkins will certainly suffer from her sharp tongue though,' he added with a chuckle. 'Thank God I am well protected from her.'

'I do believe you're serious — about Moorend, I mean. I can't say I disagree. Sinclair rarely asks for repairs if he can do them himself and he maintains things in good condition.' He smiled. 'I remember hearing about their eldest boy, Jamie, when he was learning to use the closet in the garden. His little arse was so small he nearly fell through the hole. Fortunately Polly went out to hang some clothes on the line and she heard him shouting for help. She told Joe Wright his little fists were white with the effort of holding on. William Sinclair went straight to Billy Little, the joiner, and asked him to make a new seat with one small hole and one normal. Billy made a really good job. He made a seat with three different holes and lids to fit. He made perfect circles and they are really smooth. I think Emma Sinclair was grateful to him. All her children seem to learn to be independent at an early age.'

'I expect they have to be with so many of them. Do they have room for a bathroom? I imagine that would save a lot of time hauling out the tin bath in front of the fire every week.'

'They don't have a hot water system to fill a bath, or anything else. They carry hot water from the boiler in the dairy for everything. Friday nights are for the women and girls to bathe, I heard, Saturdays for the men and boys.'

'I imagine Mrs Sinclair must be a good organizer. Anytime I've been invited to the school her children always look clean and neatly dressed.'

'She is a good organizer but I'm sure they would all appreciate an indoor water closet, at least. The dairy is so big it would be easy enough to divide it into a separate dairy with a scullery and build a water closet in one corner. That would be quick to do and it would save them all going outside on a winter's day. We could install one at Mountcliffe at the same time.'

'Aah, you're protecting your hide from Mrs Wilkins' wrath,' Lord Hanley said.

'I'm not worried about my own hide. I was thinking more about Emma Sinclair. Ma Wilkins already resents her because she didn't get Maisie Blackford as a maid. That woman has a vicious tongue. She's evil, in fact.'

'All right, you can see about installing a water closet for each of them. Once Mrs Wilkins has been mollified you could discuss the possibility of a bathroom with Sinclair.

They would benefit more than most of our tenants, but we'll try to do the same for all of them eventually.'

'I think Mrs Sinclair must have made a good impression on you the night of the tenants' dinner, m'Lord,' Bob Rowbottom remarked.

'She did. I reckon she's the type to stand beside her husband in bad times and good. Lady Hanley was quite impressed too and she's usually a good judge of character. We haven't had so much trouble with the gypsies either since they took over Moorend, have we?'

'No, and I'm grateful to William Sinclair for that. He plays fair with them. He makes good use of their labour to get in his hay and harvest but in return he makes sure they get a stack of fodder for their own animals. It seems to work well. No more cutting down fences for their firewood anyway. I believe they still do some poaching and I'll bet they take Mrs Sinclair a hare or two. She says the old gypsy, Yakira, is always wanting to tell her fortune but she tells her the same every time, mainly that young Jamie will bring her heartache.'

'Don't most children bring a little heartache at one time or another?'

'I suppose they do. I remember it took us a while to get over it when our only lass got married and moved to Ireland, but we're thankful she's alive and healthy.'

'You should tell Emma Sinclair that then, in case she's imagining all sorts of terrible disasters.'

'I will if the opportunity arises. Her husband can be a bit possessive.'

'Yes, Lady Hanley thought he might be, but you must admit she is a very attractive young woman, as well as a capable one, and a hard worker. He probably knows he wouldn't find it easy to replace her.'

'I expect that's why he married her so young. Anyway, back to other business. Wilkins is sure to ask whether installing modern conveniences to the farmhouses will put up the rents.'

'You can tell him not at present, but they can't stay the same for ever and I would like to modernise the cottages in the village eventually. We can't stand still. Times are changing since the old Queen died and transport is getting easier, so people move around more and get ideas.'

It was true Peter's birth had been a long and difficult one because he had come buttocks first. It had taken more out of Emma than usual. He was smaller than her other babies had been and not such a good feeder. Each feed took longer so he grew tired and needed small feeds more often. The winter days were short and cold; Emma struggled to cast off her low spirits. Deep down she knew it was not only a new baby and her busy household that was weighing her down. Every week since she came to Yorkshire she had written to her mother and father and she looked forward eagerly to her mother's replies. Usually these were full of news about her brothers, Richard and Davy and their wives and children and about Joe who still lived at home and seemed to have no desire to marry. He had done well in his job and been promoted to manager in the factory where he worked. Her mother's pride shone through her letters.

Recently Emma had sensed a difference though, almost a weariness, if that was possible. Certainly her letters were shorter and contained less news of people from Locheagle village. Emma felt an overwhelming urge to see both her parents again. It was ten years since her marriage to William but the time seemed to have passed like the blink of an eye. In spite of the constant work they were happy and they both derived great satisfaction from the improvements they had made at Moorend, both inside and out. Although there was always something needed for the farm, money was not quite so scarce as it had been in their early years and when William got top price for one of his Ayrshire heifers at the market he often brought her a small gift as a surprise. Emma knew she was fortunate the way her life had turned out but she could not dispel a feeling of unease. Sometimes she thought Peter sensed her mood and she wondered if it was her fault that he was less contented and didn't sleep so well as her other babies had.

The day two letters arrived together, Emma opened the one from her brother and sister-in-law first. Usually David wrote the first half leaving Julie to finish off with news of their three children and any bits of village gossip he had forgotten. Emma had never forgotten how kind and understanding Julie and her parents had been when she had returned home in disgrace as an unmarried mother. As minister of the parish, Julie's father had given her every support and consideration, conducting her marriage to William and christening Jamie, when others had condemned her for the shame she had brought to her family. So she was surprised when Julie's letter began by asking her forgiveness if what she had to say caused Emma unnecessary anxiety.

David does not know I am writing, and he may blame me for taking on this task without his approval. The truth is, dear Emma, we are all deeply concerned about your mother's health. You know she never complains and she still summons a smile when we ask how she is feeling but she has lost a lot of weight and she is constantly tired. She has deteriorated more rapidly these past two months. Perhaps as a vicar's daughter, I ought not to write this but if I was a long distance away and could not see my mother for myself, I should want to know if she was ill. I would prefer to visit while she is able to see me and speak to me, rather than making a supreme effort to travel to her funeral.

Emma gasped at the word 'funeral'. She knew Julie would not have written this without being very sure that such a thing was looming. She had gone on to say she understood how busy Emma's life must be with another young baby and all her other children to care for, as well as workers to feed and look after and cows to milk. She had offered to accommodate any of the children if she wanted to bring them, adding she was sure it would make his granny very happy if she could see Jamie again as she had mentioned him frequently lately. Once more she begged Emma's forgiveness if she was adding an impossible burden.

Emma sat for a long time, staring into space, longing to jump on a train immediately and go to see her mother for herself, to throw her arms around her, to talk to her . . . Yet how could she go and leave her household, the children, William, the cooking and washing, the care of the men?

Eventually she remembered the letter from Maggie. As soon as she began to read she realized William's sister must have been down at Locheagle and discussed her and her family with Julie.

I can imagine how difficult it must be for you to leave your responsibilities, but I agreed with Julie that we ought to tell you the truth about your mother's health. We both know she will not have told you herself. If there is any chance of you coming, however brief your stay, I will meet you at the station with the pony and trap, and take you back again for your return journey. I understand better than most how difficult it must be to take time away from your home and children, even though I do not have children of my own. Mother is as demanding as a child these days.

It was the first time Maggie had made the slightest criticism of her mother, or mentioned her own circumstances. She always wrote cheerfully giving them news of Jim and her father at Bonnybrae and William's married brother and sisters.

That evening, William drew her aside in the dairy when she would have hurried after Polly into the kitchen to serve their evening meal.

'Emma, what's the matter?' he asked. 'All day I have felt there is something troubling you. Are you ill? I know wee Peter tires you more than usual.' He sounded so anxious that Emma's eyes filled with unexpected tears at his concern. He pulled her into his arms and held her close, wiping her tears away with a gentle finger. 'I knew something was troubling you, Emmie. Please tell me. Maybe I can help?'

'I had letters from Julie and from Maggie today . . . But, William, the men are hungry and waiting for their food . . .'

'Bugger the men for once. What did the letters say to distress you so?'

'It's my mother. She — she is ill. I will show you the letters when we have eaten.'

'Show them to me now. The news has obviously upset you very much, dearest Emmie. I will read them while you serve the food and attend to the children.'

As soon as he had read Julie's letter, William was filled with remorse. He should have made sure Emma visited her parents long before now. He would make arrangements for her to go home to Scotland without delay. He prayed there was still time for her to see her mother. She would be nervous at the prospect of the long train journey and he longed to go with her. He would like to see Jim and Maggie and his father again too, but he knew it was impossible for both of them to be away. They couldn't leave the children and the animals, the milking and all the work inside and out. Polly and Tom were conscientious but so much responsibility was asking too much of them. Cliff Barnes was a willing fellow, strong and hard-working, but he could be a liability and unwittingly do serious damage in a matter of seconds if he was not constantly supervised. William sighed. There was nothing for it but to let Emma go alone. As soon as they were alone, he insisted Emma must go to Scotland without delay.

'I couldn't leave the baby,' Emma said at once. 'Peter seems to need more attention and feeds than normal and Polly and Maisie will have their hands full with the rest of the children and the cooking and washing.'

'Julie thinks your mother would like to see Jamie. Maybe he could help with the luggage? I hate the idea of you going on your own Emmie, but . . .'

'Hush,' she said softly, putting a finger to his lips. 'I wish you could come too but I know we can't both be spared. I had considered taking Meg. She's a good wee nursemaid and she loves to cuddle Peter.'

'All right. Take Jamie and Meg to help with the baby and the luggage. I know you will need extra things for wee Peter. I remember when we brought Jamie as a baby.'

Emma was too nervous and excited to sleep well and it was a great relief when William insisted he would take them to Wakefield and see them on the train for Scotland. He had sent a telegram to let Maggie know when they expected to arrive at Kilmarnock so she would have an idea what time to meet them. Meg and Jamie were full of excitement at the prospect of travelling so far by rail. They were pleased to be missing school, but Allan and John wanted to go on the train too and it upset Emma when they alternated between tears and being naughty. Wee Marie, at only thirteen months old, was too young to understand what was happening and she had grown used to Polly looking after her since Peter was born. Maisie Blackford had agreed to stay at Moorend until Emma returned, and with her usual calm efficiency she had cleared away the breakfast, made a parcel of sandwiches and packed some shortbread and two bottles of buttermilk.

'I would have liked to take butter and eggs for my parents,' Emma said to William, 'but it's impossible to carry everything. I'm taking a piece of ham to boil but it has made my case quite heavy.'

'I'll help you, Mam,' Jamie said quickly, proud to be the man in charge since his father had explained he could not go with them.

'I can carry some butter,' Meg offered, not to be outdone by her brother.

'Well, maybe a wee bit, then, if we wrap it up twice and then in cotton,' Emma agreed, giving her young daughter a hug.

Maggie was waiting at the little station to greet them. Her face was unlined and pleasant as ever but Emma got a shock when she saw her thick black hair had turned snowy white where it peeped beneath her hat. Maggie was the only one of all the Sinclairs who had had raven dark hair. It had always been thick and glossy and turned into a mass of curls if she was out in the rain or standing in the steam in the wash house. They hugged each other and Emma couldn't hold back a few tears.

‘It’s so good to see you,’ Maggie said, smiling at them all. ‘And can this fine young man be Jamie?’

‘Yes, I am Jamie.’

‘The last time I saw you, you were a baby, about the same as your wee brother, and now you’re almost as tall as your mother.’ She turned to give Meg a warm hug. ‘And you are my wee namesake. We’re both christened Margaret, even though everyone calls us something different. I’m your Aunt Maggie and I’m delighted to see you at last.’ Maggie looked up at Emma over her head. ‘My father and Jim would really like to see you all, if it’s possible.’ She settled them and their luggage in the trap and Emma sat up at the front beside her, holding a sleepy Peter tightly in her arms.

‘You must be prepared for a shock, Emma,’ Maggie said in a low voice. ‘Your mother has grown very frail recently. I know she will be so very happy when she sees you.’ Emma nodded, swallowing the lump in her throat with difficulty.

‘Julie and David offered to keep the children but . . .’

‘I know they did but your father and Joe want them to stay with them. Joe says Jamie can have Richard’s bed beside him upstairs and your father thought Meg could share your old room. Julie has loaned them a cot for the baby. Will that be all right?’ she asked anxiously. ‘I think your father wants to make the most of your stay. He is so pleased you have come.’

‘I don’t mind where we sleep. I’m just so happy to be here,’ Emma said huskily. ‘How are your own parents, and Jim?’

‘Father has aged a lot but ten years is a long time. He really missed William. So did Jim. It was Mother, and her stupid pride, who insisted he should leave the district of course.’ Maggie’s soft mouth hardened. ‘I’m afraid she has grown more difficult and very demanding. Even Father has grown tired of humouring her.’

‘I am so sorry to hear that,’ Emma said. Then, lowering her voice, ‘I know it was all my fault but I knew so little then. I had no idea it was so easy to have babies and I truly didn’t know I was expecting when . . .’

'Hush, Emmie,' Maggie said softly, moving one hand from the reins to pat Emma's arm. 'If anyone was at fault it was William, but I know he didn't intend to bring shame to your family or his own. We all thought Mother was being too harsh but . . .' She bit her lip. 'She still has not forgiven him in spite of all her quoting from the Bible. I don't know how she can be so bitter. You are happy together, aren't you?'

'Oh yes. I didn't want to move so far away but my life has turned out better than I could have dreamed. I think William is happy too. He yearns to prove he is a success without his family's help or influence. I know Mr Rowbottom, our land agent, respects his knowledge and hard work. I think Lord Hanley must do too because he has extended our lease on Moorend.'

'I'm glad. Emmie.' Maggie hesitated. 'You should be prepared for a shock when you see the change in your mother,' Maggie repeated. 'She was such a strong person, always busy, yet ready with a cup of tea. I have enjoyed visiting her since you went away and it saddens me to see the change.'

'Thank you, Maggie,' Emma said softly, 'and thank you for meeting us at the station.' She looked behind to see Meg and Jamie gazing round-eyed as they drew into Locheagle. 'That's where I went to school,' she told them, pointing to the grey stone building set back from the road.

Although Maggie had tried to prepare her, Emma struggled to hide her dismay at the frail, shrunken figure of her mother, but there was no doubting the joy they both felt at being together again. Emma passed baby Peter to Maggie and knelt beside the box bed to hug her mother close, but she was made even more aware of how small and fragile she had become. Her bones seemed as delicate as those of a little bird.

'Oh, Ma you should have told me you were ill! I should have come sooner.'

'There was nothing you could have done, lassie, nothing anyone can do, but there's no denying it fills my old heart with joy to see you again.' She drew away gently and looked at Meg and Jamie. 'And these are such fine children you have,

Emma. I can't believe this fine laddie is the wee Jamie you held in your arms when you went away. And this is Meg? Eh lassie, your mother has told me a lot about you in her letters and what a good wee nursemaid you are.'

'Hello lassie, it's fair grand to see ye,' Bert Greig said, joining Emma on the hearthrug and hugging her tightly. 'I've put the kettle on. You and Maggie will be ready for a cup of tea.'

'This is your Grandfather Greig. Come and say hello, Jamie, and you too Meg.' The children responded readily to the warmth of these welcoming people. The only other family they knew were the Kerrs from Blaketop and they were not close relations. Emma saw that her father had aged too but she understood how worried he must be about her mother. Emma never remembered them quarrelling when she had lived at home. Maggie and Emma were grateful for the cup of hot tea but Bert knew his wife would not take any. Even tea seemed to upset her these last few days. He wondered how much longer she could go on. He didn't want to lose her but it made his heart ache to see her wasting away. He thanked God Emma had managed to visit before it was too late. He guessed Julie and Maggie must have arranged things between them.

'I would like to hold the baby,' Eliza said, holding out her arms. Maggie gently lowered Peter into the crook of her arm. 'What a good wee fellow he is, coming all this way to see his old granny.'

'Ah-ah,' Emma warned. 'He is not usually so good. I dreaded the journey but the movement of the train seemed to agree with him.'

'It did,' Meg chirruped happily. 'He never cried once and he slept nearly all the time. Can we go and bring the bag from the trap, Mam?' she asked, remembering they had buttermilk and shortbread left. 'Will the pony stand still?'

'Yes, he will,' Maggie smiled. 'He's very quiet and I tied him to the gate and gave him a wee bag of hay.'

'Shall I bring in some of our other bags, Mam?' Jamie asked. Emma nodded.

'Is that what they call you? "Mam"?' Bert Greig asked.

'It's what most of the children call their mothers where we live.' Emma smiled. 'We've had to get used to a lot of words stranger than that.'

'I'll cut some cake,' Bert Greig said, bringing a large sponge cake from the little pantry. 'Julie brought it, and some biscuits and scones.' He was not used to household chores but he did his best. 'She's a grand lassie and a good wife to Davy.'

'Yes, we're well blessed,' Eliza agreed. 'Joe has done well at his work but I just wish he could have settled down with a nice homely wife.' Emma was surprised to see a faint blush stain Maggie's fair skin. She couldn't get used to her white hair. It made her seem older than her years. She was even more surprised when Joe arrived home half an hour later.

'You're finished early today, laddie,' Bert Greig greeted his eldest son.

'There's no point in being the boss if I can't get time to see my wee sister when she comes all this way to visit.' Joe grinned and seized Emma round her waist, swinging her off her feet as he used to do. Meg giggled at the sight of her mother being lifted like a child. Jamie grinned widely at the sight of his mother's flustered face. Joe whispered in her ear, his voice husky, 'I'm glad you've come in time, Emmie.' He set her on her feet and turned to his mother. 'I'm having a few days off while Emma is here, Mother. I want to get to know my niece and nephew.'

'Oh Joe, it is good to see you again,' Emma said tremulously. 'This is your Uncle Joe, Jamie and Meg. You're looking well, Joe.' He smiled.

'I can't grumble. I know you will not be able to stay long so Maggie and I thought we might take these two rascals to the seaside for a picnic tomorrow, to give you and Mother a bit of peace together.' He turned to the children. 'Would you like that? We would need to go on the train to get to Ayr.'

'We've never seen the sea!'

'We'd love that, wouldn't we Meg?' Jamie said excitedly. Emma looked at Maggie in surprise. It seemed she was on very friendly terms with Joe.

'Will that be all right? I mean can you spare the time to — to leave Bonnybrae?'

'Yes.' Maggie's mouth tightened. 'You really mean can I leave my mother? I have arranged for Mrs Edgar to come in more often while you are here. Jim and my father seem to think it will do me good to have a day away.' She looked at Joe and smiled. There was a softness on her face which Emma had never seen before and Joe responded with a gentle look and a nod.

'Jim and Father would love to see you and the children but they understand you will want to spend as much time as you can with your mother. Maybe they could call in to say hello? Mother will not be happy,' she said with a grimace. 'She never is these days, whatever we do to please her. She gets confused and that makes her angry.'

'We'd be happy for your father and Jim to call on us here, wouldn't we Eliza?' Bert Greig assured Maggie. Emma was pleased to see her mother nod and summon a smile.

'Of course they're welcome, lassie. Emma will be here to make them a cup of tea and a bite to eat.' Emma smiled and nodded at Maggie.

'I would like to see them, and William will be pleased, but it would suit me better than taking time to go to Bonnybrae.'

'That's good. I shall tell them. They may even come this evening if you're not too tired?' She glanced at Joe. He understood how bitter and difficult her mother had become, but they didn't want Emma to know she still would not welcome her at Bonnybrae.

Emma went to sit beside her mother where she lay in the box bed on one side of the fireplace. The curtains were drawn back during the day so it was almost like a settee, but Emma's heart felt heavy seeing how weak her robust little mother had become. She had not risen from it since they arrived. Joe noticed how weary she looked after her joyful anticipation of seeing her only daughter again.

'Are you bairns any good at walking?' he asked with a grin, looking at his nephew and niece.'

'Of course we are, Uncle Joe,' Meg said, puffing out her little chest.

'We walk to school every morning and back home again at night.' Jamie said.

'And how far is that?'

'Two miles and a bit. That's because our farm is right at the far end of Silverbeck and the school is at the other end of the village.'

'All right. What do you say if we go with Maggie in the pony and trap to see your other grandfather and Uncle Jim, then we would have to walk three miles back here. I expect you would be glad to stretch your young legs and have freedom to run after sitting on the train for so long?'

'Oh yes, we'd love that, wouldn't we, Meg?'

'Yes. We had to sit still and not fidget when other people got into our railway carriage. We were good, weren't we Mam?'

'You were indeed,' Emma smiled. 'Will that be all right, Maggie? I would like them to see where their father used to live.'

'My father will be really pleased to see them. Jamie is very like a picture we have when Father was a young man. He has the same colouring with the slightly reddish tinge to his hair. All my family have that colouring, except me. Meg, you have lovely dark hair like your mother. Mine used to be even darker than that.'

CHAPTER FOUR

When Maggie drove the pony and trap into the farmyard her father and brother Jim were standing outside the byre talking to one of the men. Her father, James Sinclair, came across to them immediately, his face wreathed in smiles of welcome as he lifted Meg and swung her into the air before setting her on her feet, while Jim instructed the man to deal with the pony and trap.

'So you are young Meg? I'm glad to see ye, lassie.' He turned to Jamie. 'There's no prizes for guessing who you are, young man,' he said as he solemnly shook the hand that Jamie had extended politely. 'You're the image of your father.'

'Joe and I think he's very like you, Father,' Maggie said.

'Oh look! Look, Uncle Joe, there's two little lambs in that pen,' Meg said excitedly and ran across to the shed to see the lambs more closely. Joe and Jim followed, smiling at her pleasure.

'I thought you had sheep?' Joe said.

'We don't have any lambs. We have baby calves and they're lovely too,' Meg said. 'I help Polly to feed them. We have two collie pups as well. Queenie was their grandmother.' She lowered her voice. 'She followed Jamie everywhere. Mother said it was because they had both come to

Moorend together. It made him very sad when she died,' she said solemnly. 'I love all babies.'

'So why don't you have sheep?' James Sinclair asked as he and Jamie joined them beside the lambs. 'Your father used to like the sheep.'

'He says Moorend has not enough acres to have breeding sheep as well as all the cows he wants to keep,' Jamie told him seriously. 'We get different sheep every year from the hills. They graze on the common. Father looks after them and keeps count, and sometimes the gypsies help too. At the end of the summer, Father sends them back to their owners and they pay him for feeding and looking after them.'

'I see,' his grandfather nodded. 'These two lambs are a bit early so we're feeding them with a bottle. Would you like to feed them?'

'Oh I would,' Meg said eagerly.

'I'd better go inside and see how Mother is and let Mrs Edgar get away home,' Maggie said.

'All right lassie. We'll be in when these two have fed the pet lambs. Everything has gone fine so don't listen to any grumbles. Mrs Edgar has the patience of a saint.'

Joe and Jim chatted amicably as they watched the children and the lambs. They had become friends over the years, since Emma's wedding to William. Jim understood Joe's reluctance to go into the house. His mother had carried a grudge against the Greig family ever since she discovered Emma was expecting William's child and he was going to marry her. Three years ago she had suffered a slight apoplexy and her tongue was sharper than ever. Jim felt she made the most of ill health to keep Maggie tied to her side. She bitterly resented Maggie's friendship with the Greigs — and especially with Emma's brother, Joe.

Eventually James Sinclair led his two grandchildren indoors, leaving the two men chatting.

'I saw Maggie making some butterscotch toffee this morning,' he said. 'Come and wash your hands and maybe she'll let you try a piece. Then you can say hello to your Grandma Sinclair. How was your Grandma Greig today?'

'She looks very ill,' Jamie said seriously, 'but she is ever so pleased we've come to see her. She says she knew me when I was a baby, like Peter.'

'And Mam and Granny Greig hugged and they both had tears in their eyes,' Meg said, 'but they said they were tears of joy at seeing each other again.'

'Aye, I expect they were, lassie,' James Sinclair said gravely. He was thankful Emma had come to see her mother before it was too late. Whatever his wife might think, the Greigs were a decent God-fearing family with none of the bitterness in their hearts which seemed to have soured her own. She never used to miss attending the kirk on a Sunday, but she had not entered its doors since William was married.

Maggie was alone in the big kitchen when they went in.

'Mother is in the room. Shall I take Jamie and Meg to see her?' she asked doubtfully.

'Of course she'll want to see them,' James said. 'They're our grandchildren. I told them you had made some butter-scotch toffee for them to eat on their way home. Joe said he wouldn't come in. He's talking to Jim. I think we'll go down to Locheagle tonight. Joe was saying he doesn't think his mother has much time left.'

'I'm sure he's right,' Maggie said quietly. 'Come on you two, dry your hands and come into the room with me.' The two children followed her, expecting another smiling welcome from another granny they had never seen before.

Mary Sinclair sat in her straight-backed chair beside the fire. She was wearing a black dress with a black brooch at the neck. Her white hair was tightly scraped back from her gaunt face and pinned in a small bun. Jamie thought she looked even more stern than Mr Thorpe, the schoolmaster, back home. Meg loved to read and she had a vivid imagination, so she felt a little afraid of this grim-faced old woman who looked like a witch, except she wasn't wearing a tall black hat.

Jamie held out his hand in greeting, as his mother had told him this was a polite way to greet his elders. The old woman ignored it. She glared at him.

'So, you bastard, you've come back.'

'Mother!' Maggie gasped aloud. Meg stepped back nervously and felt Maggie behind her. She clutched a handful of her aunt's skirt and looked up at her, her sea-green eyes wide and round, reminding Maggie of Emma when she had first come to Bonnybrae.

'My — my name is Jamie, ma'am. Jamie Sinclair,' Jamie offered politely. 'I — we, we — are your g-grandchildren.'

'You're a bastard, that's what you are. You're not a Sinclair. Your name is Greig. It has to be.'

'Come along with me, Jamie,' Maggie said firmly. She gave Meg's small hand a reassuring squeeze, her eyes filled with disgust. 'Mother has been ill. She's confused. She doesn't realize what she's saying,' she said as she ushered them back to the kitchen but not before Mary Sinclair almost spat the words. 'I'm not confused. He was born out of wedlock and that makes . . .' Maggie closed the door, shutting out her words but her face was pale. Her father was standing in front of the fire and he raised his eyebrows questioningly at their quick exit. Maggie shook her head, her mouth tightening but Jamie turned to her, his young face hurt and puzzled.

'That old woman didn't want to see us, did she? What is a bastard? I'm sure Dad told Cliff Barnes it is a bad word.' James Sinclair winced and frowned.

'She behaved like a naughty child ' Maggie muttered. He nodded, understanding.

'Your grandma is getting old,' he said with a sigh. 'She doesn't know what she's saying.' He smiled at their anxious young faces. 'Come and taste some of Maggie's toffee. Does your mother make toffee for you?'

'She makes treacle toffee on Bonfire Night, and ginger cake called parkin,' Meg offered, selecting a piece of the golden coloured sweet which her aunt had set out on a plate. Maggie left the children with her father and hurried outside to warn Joe and her brother about her mother's shameful outburst.

'I'd better take them away home,' Joe said. 'Maybe I shouldn't have brought them here. I hope the wee laddie is not upset?'

'You did right to bring them, Joe,' said Jim. 'They're William's bairns and my father is genuinely glad to see them. So am I. Our mother is getting more difficult every day. I don't understand her. She used to be so dignified and polite, even to people she didn't like. That apoplexy must have affected her brain, although the doctor said it was mild.'

'I think Jamie might ask questions,' Maggie said. 'I'll wrap up some toffee for them to eat on the way home but he's a bright laddie and I doubt if he'll forget. We shall have to make sure they enjoy their day with us tomorrow, Joe.'

'I reckon we shall all enjoy it, Maggie,' Joe said with his warm smile. 'I'm looking forward to it myself.'

'Yes, so am I,' Maggie agreed, but a faint colour stained her cheeks as she glanced at Jim. He winked at her.

'You deserve a day away from this place, or at least from your duties caring for Mother. She has kept you bound to her side too long. I hope you both enjoy the day.'

Joe thought the children were quieter on the way home, or perhaps they were tired after the excitement of the long train journey and meeting so many relations they had never seen before. They certainly enjoyed Maggie's toffee and he was relieved Jamie didn't ask him to explain why his grandmother had called him a bastard. Although it was a three-mile walk to Locheagle, Joe had always enjoyed it when he and Richard or Davy had come to meet Emma on her day off once a month when she started working at Bonnybrae as a young maid. She had been so innocent. He couldn't understand how that old woman could be so bitter and unforgiving. Jim had told him it was her idea to get William out of the district so he didn't bring shame to her door, but she had not bargained for him returning to marry Emma and take her with him as his wife. It was unfortunate that Jamie had already been born before the marriage could take place.

As soon as they entered his parents' cottage, Joe could smell baking. It was a long time since his mother had had the strength for anything that needed effort, or standing for more than a few moments.

'Mmm, lovely. I see you've been baking scones, Emmie,' he said with a grin.

'It seems strange to be baking again back here,' Emma smiled. 'But Mother has had a nice wee sleep so I thought I would get on with baking. You have no idea how much these two can eat. We brought a piece of ham so I'm just cooking it and Meg brought some butter. We would have liked to bring more but we couldn't carry everything.'

'Eh, lassie, so long as you and the bairns have come that's all I wanted,' her mother said from the box bed in the corner. 'I count myself well blessed now to see you here and to be able to talk. You write a grand letter, lassie. I've kept them all, but nothing can beat seeing you again.' Joe looked at his father. That was the longest speech his mother had managed for weeks. Even talking seemed to sap her energy. His father smiled and nodded at him.

'Our Emmie always brought a ray of sunshine into the house. And how did you two get on meeting your Grandfather Sinclair?' he asked. 'And your Uncle Jim?'

'They were pleased to see us and Grandfather said I look like Dad,' Jamie said.

'They let us feed two pet lambs,' Meg joined in excitedly, her face wreathed in smiles, 'and Auntie Maggie made some lovely toffee for us. We saved a piece for you. Mam.' She produced a piece of toffee wrapped in paper from her pinafore pocket. 'We didn't like the old woman though. She was a witch except she didn't have a black pointed hat . . .'

'Oh hush, Meggie!' Emma said drawing Meg to her. 'You mustn't say that about your Grandma Sinclair. She is your Dad's mother.'

'Well, she wasn't like Grandma Greig. She didn't want to see us. I told her my name was Jamie Sinclair but she said I was a bastard and my name should be Greig.' Emma gasped and her face paled. In the box bed her mother stirred as she tried to sit up again. Emma went to her at once and propped her on a mound of pillows. 'Don't listen, Mother. She doesn't know what she's saying,' she urged, afraid her mother would get upset. She saw her father's mouth had tightened angrily.

'Come on laddie, we'll take your bag upstairs so you can unpack your things while your mother makes the tea.'

'That would be a good idea,' Emma said cheerfully. 'Maybe you could unpack yours in the bedroom, Meg. Through here. Wee Peter has been ever so good. He slept all the time you were away beside Grandma Greig.' As soon as they were in the bedroom, Meg turned to her mother.

'It's true, Mam, what Jamie said. She did call him that name and Jamie was upset because he had heard Dad say it is a bad word.'

'Well, we'll talk about it when we get back home, but not here. It upsets Grandma Greig to hear bad words. Will you tell Jamie that too? Now, are you looking forward to going to the seaside with Uncle Joe tomorrow?'

'Oh, yes we are! Did you hear somebody? I think somebody has come.'

'It sounds like Uncle Davy and Aunt Julia,' Emma said. 'Finish unpacking then come and say hello.' Meg hastily emptied her bag of clothes onto the bed and hurried after her mother in time to see yet another new uncle lift her mother in the air as though she was no more than a rag doll.

'Oh Davy, put me down!' Emma squealed, but Meg saw she was laughing with joy. This was the uncle and aunt who wrote letters almost every week. 'I can't believe how strong and broad you've grown since I last saw you,' Emma said. He set her on her feet and she turned to hug her sister-in-law. 'You must be feeding him too well, dearest Julie.'

'We thought we would call in for a very short visit before you settle down for the evening,' Julie said, smiling as she caught sight of Meg. 'We have not brought the children but they will be so pleased to see you, Meg, and you too, Jamie. They want to hear all about your farm and the animals.'

'Uncle Joe and Aunt Maggie are taking us to the seaside tomorrow,' Meg said shyly, 'but we'll still have one more day to come and play.'

'Joe and Maggie are taking you?' Davy whistled and looked at his elder brother with raised eyebrows, his grey eyes dancing with mischief. 'Well, they do say it's never too late . . .'

'Watch it, little brother!' Joe warned but he was smiling. Emma turned to where her mother lay propped up in the box bed. She was smiling serenely.

'It's lovely to see you all together again,' she murmured as she caught Emma's eye. 'I expect Richard and Annie will be in after they've eaten their meal.'

'I should think these two rogues are tired out,' Bert Greig said. 'They've had a long journey and a walk back from Bonnybrae with Joe. I'll bet you never expected to see so many relations, did you, bairns?'

'No, but Dad will be pleased we've seen you all,' Jamie said. 'When Mam gets a letter he always asks for the news from Scotland before she has finished reading.'

'That's true,' Emma said with a smile. 'I never thought you noticed such things, Jamie.'

'We like all our new family except the old woman like a witch,' Meg said with all the honesty of childhood. 'We don't think she liked us either, do we, Jamie?'

'Well she wasn't pleased to see us,' he agreed, frowning. 'She called me a bastard. I know Dad thinks that's a bad word because he said I hadn't to repeat it.' Emma bit hard on her lower lip when she saw Davy's mouth purse in a silent whistle.

'Oh my dear boy,' her mother said sadly, shaking her white head in sorrow.

'Maybe I shouldn't have taken them up there,' Joe said uneasily, 'but their grandfather and Jim were really pleased to see them and they're coming down to see Emma this evening.'

'You did the right thing to take them,' Julie said firmly. 'Such a bitter heart can't hold much happiness. I thought Mrs Sinclair was supposed to be a devout Christian. Where is her mercy?'

'Maggie says she never goes to the kirk these days,' Joe said. 'Mind you, she can't get around very well now. She uses two sticks since she had her apoplexy, but even before that she had stopped attending.'

'How strange,' Julie murmured, 'but perhaps her faith was not as sincere as she pretended. I'm sure my father would say the loss is hers. We're all so happy to see you, Emma, and so pleased you could bring three of the children. Peter seems to be a very contented baby.'

'That's the strange thing — he's not usually very good at all. I think it is Mother's magic touch which is soothing him.'

'But he was good on the train too, Mam,' Meg said loyally, 'and you said you were dreading the journey with him.'

'That's true. The movement seemed to rock him to sleep and even the jolts and noises didn't disturb him.'

Emma set out their evening meal when Davy and Julie insisted they must get back to their children. It was with a heavy heart she saw her mother ate only the smallest morsel of food. A little water seemed to be the only drink she was able to keep down, even though she had always enjoyed a good cup of tea. No wonder she was so thin and tired. The effort of eating at all seemed to have exhausted her and she fell into a doze before her father and the children had finished eating. Emma met her father's gaze. He shook his head sadly and she knew he accepted that her mother's time was very limited indeed.

'I'm so glad I've come,' she said softly, 'although there is nothing I can do.'

'Aah lassie, your coming has been the best gift we could have wished for. I'm glad Julie and Maggie had the good sense to tell ye how things are.'

'So am I,' Emma said fervently. Meg helped her clear their meal away and wash the dishes in the small scullery off the kitchen. Both Jamie and Meg were tired and needed no persuading to get ready for bed. It had been a long, exciting day and they were looking forward to more excitement tomorrow. Emma was exhausted herself, but she had just finished feeding and changing Peter when James Sinclair and Jim arrived.

'Hello Emma, it's good to see you,' Jim leaned forward and kissed her cheek. 'We saw Richard as we rode past his house. He says he and Annie will wait until tomorrow evening to see you and the children. He thinks you will have had enough visitors for one day. Perhaps we should have waited too.'

'No, no, we're pleased to see ye both,' Bert Greig said, pulling forward two more chairs to the fireside while James Sinclair shook Emma's hand, then unexpectedly drew her to him in a hug.

'Eh lassie but I'm pleased to see ye,' he said huskily. 'Ye're even bonnier than ye were as a young lassie, in spite of all the work you must have with your family and helping William.' Emma hadn't realized how tense she had been at the prospect of meeting her father-in-law again but there was no doubting the warmth of his greeting, or that he seemed pleased to see her. She began to relax a little. In the box bed, her mother stirred and opened her eyes.

'Oh dear, how bad mannered I am to fall asleep when we have company,' she murmured. She summoned her usual gentle smile and greeted her visitors. Emma saw James Sinclair swallow hard before he bent to greet her mother, then she remembered he had been at school with her parents and it must be a shock to see how frail her sturdy, bustling mother had become.

Both he and Jim plied her with questions about William, Moorend Farm and their landlord, the stock they had, the Clydesdales and collies.

'William thinks Jamie will be good at training the collie dogs, if only we had sheep all year round for him to keep practising. He loves horses and dogs much more than milking cows.'

'Does he now? Well we have plenty of sheep up here and we could do with a good dog trainer.' James Sinclair sighed heavily.

'William was always the best at training the dogs,' Jim said. 'Maybe Jamie has inherited his patience.' He and his father refused to let her make tea.

'We'd rather talk to you, and hear about your family while we have the chance. I see you have another fine wee fellow here too,' her father-in-law smiled, leaning forward to stroke Peter's soft cheek. 'That must be four sons and two daughters you have now?'

'That's right,' Emma smiled. 'Lord Hanley and Mr Rowbottom tease William. They think he's aiming to produce a tenant for all the farms on the estate.'

'Mr Rowbottom? Is he the factor then? You get on well with him?'

'He's called the land agent down there. His main concern is that tenants pay the rent on time and don't make too many demands. Apparently not all the tenants do pay promptly. Mr Rowbottom told me William is the best tenant he has when it comes to maintaining things himself, like the doors and windows and small building repairs. We think that's why Lord Hanley agreed to double the size of our cowshed so we could keep more cows.' Out of the corner of her eye she saw her father rise and go to the cupboard where he kept a bottle of whisky. Both he and her mother had always been hospitable. She went to the dresser and brought out four glasses.

'You'll drink a dram with Joe and me,' her father said, pouring a generous tot of whisky for James and Jim and a smaller one for Joe and himself. 'Can I get anything for you, Emma?'

'No, thank you.' She shook her head.

'Go on, lassie, you were saying the landlord made you a bigger byre?'

'We asked for that and he agreed. His latest idea is a real surprise. We would never have dreamed of asking him. We have a huge scullery, combined with a wash house and the dairy. He is dividing it into two rooms. One half will be the dairy, the other half a scullery, and off the scullery he is building a small room and installing a water closet for us. We shall not need to go down the garden in the rain or the dark anymore.'

'A water closet?' Jim looked at his father. 'None of the tenants on our estate have water closets yet, do they?'

'Not that I've heard of. It seems all the hard work is paying off for the pair o' ye,' James Sinclair said. 'It's a great relief to me to hear things seem to be going so well. I always knew the pair of ye were hard workers but it's not easy to make a new start amongst strangers. I've bitterly regretted sending William away.' He looked at Bert Greig, the old friend from his school days. 'We never thought our families would be united, did we? I should never have listened to Mary. People would soon have forgotten once they were married.'

'Some people never forget, or forgive, James.' They all turned towards the box bed in surprise at the sound of Eliza's low voice. She gave a wan smile. 'I've been listening even though my eyes are closed. I'm proud o' them both, James, and their family. You should be too. Life's too short for regrets.'

'Aye, ye're right there, Lizzie. You were never very big but you always had more wisdom in your curly head than the rest o' us when we were at the school.'

'I think we ought to be leaving now, Father,' Jim said. 'Emma has had a long day. How long can you stay, Emmie?'

'Two clear days, then we'll travel home on Thursday,' Emma said. 'You're sure it will be all right for Maggie to take a whole day off tomorrow? Meg and Jamie are really excited about seeing the sea.'

'It will do Maggie and Joe as much good as the bairns,' James Sinclair said firmly. 'They're her nephew and niece, aye, and Joe's. It will be good for all of them.'

Emma went to the door with her father to bid them good night. She was surprised when her father-in-law turned back and hugged her again, seizing the opportunity to whisper in her ear, 'I'm sorry William's mother called Jamie a bastard. She doesn't know what she's saying sometimes. Her heart's full o' bile and neither William nor you are the cause, and certainly not your bairns. I'm proud o' you both.'

'Then maybe you will come to visit us one day? I know it would please William.'

'I would like that. Maybe I will, some day.' He didn't need to tell her he would never come while his wife was alive.

CHAPTER FIVE

Although the early March weather was cold it was dry and sunny, so Jamie and Meg thoroughly enjoyed their visit to the seaside. Emma got the impression that Maggie and Joe had enjoyed it too, although for different reasons. It pleased her to think that her brother and Maggie had become such good friends. Joe had bought a big ball and he and Maggie had both enjoyed playing with the children on the sands. Later, he had bought a bucket and spade and Meg giggled when she told Emma he and Maggie had sat in one of the shelters and watched while they made a sand castle and filled the moat with water. Then they had raced along the sand to get warm before the tide came in.

'We gathered lots of shells. This one is for you, Granny, because it is the prettiest one. Shall I set it on the hearth so that you can see it?'

'Aye you do that, lassie. It is pretty.' Emma saw her mother's eyes were bright with tears but she blinked them away.

'Uncle Joe says you can hear the sea if you hold it close to your ear but I think he's teasing us,' Meg chattered on. 'Jamie brought you a lovely pebble too.'

'Here it is, Granny.' Jamie fished it out of his pocket. 'See how smooth and white it is. It's nearly perfect.' He set it on the hearth beside Meg's shell.

'What lovely bairns you are,' Eliza said softly. 'Come closer so I can give you both a hug to say thank you. Do you know I've never seen the sea?'

'Maybe Uncle Joe will take you too when you get better,' Meg said innocently.

'Aye, maybe he will, lassie.'

The fresh air and games had tired them out so they were ready for bed by the time Richard and Annie and their two children came that evening. They played together for a little while but Emma ushered them both to bed when she saw them yawning and rubbing their eyes.

'I think the fresh air and exercise must have tired me too,' Joe grinned, also stifling a yawn, 'but it was a good day.'

'Are you sure it was the bairns who tired you out?' Richard teased. 'I never thought I'd see the day when you were walking out with a woman.' Joe merely smiled. Emma was intrigued and surprised. Was it possible that Maggie and Joe were more than just good friends and companions? Mrs Sinclair would never agree even to friendship if she knew. Maggie was nearly ten years older than William so she must be about forty-three. She had thought Maggie was too tied to her mother to fall in love and marry and now she was too old. She was one of the sweetest people Emma knew so surely she deserved someone to love, and to love her in return, however old she was. She counted in her head, working out Joe's age. He and Richard were the oldest, then her mother had lost two babies before she had Davy. At twenty-seven, she was the youngest. That made Joe about thirty-seven.

'Your thoughts were miles away, Emma,' Richard teased. She smiled at him. He had always been very protective of her when she was at home but he had still been at the walking out stage with Annie when she married William and left Locheagle, so Emma had never known her as well as she knew

Davy's wife, Julie. Neither Richard nor Annie wrote letters very often but they seemed genuinely pleased to see her. They didn't stay late because their children needed to get to bed too and Richard could see how weary his mother looked.

'I'm glad you came, Emma,' he said quietly when he bid her goodnight. 'She always reads your letters at least three times and gives us your news. I believe she's saved them all but she was really happy when she knew you were coming. It's perked her up no end.'

'Has it?' That made Emma wonder how much worse her mother could have been a few days earlier.

Emma was not sure what had wakened her. Her bedroom was in darkness and she didn't want to light the candle in case she disturbed Meg or Peter. She lay tense, listening; then she knew. Her mother was suffering a spasm of violent coughing. She groped for her shawl, which she always laid on a chair beside the bed ready to attend to any of the children. She crept out of the room. The lamp was still burning in the kitchen and embers of fire glowed in the grate. Her father was sitting on the edge of the box bed, one arm around her mother's thin shoulders, holding her. In his other hand he held the chamber pot. Emma's eyes widened in shock. 'Blood?' Her lips formed the question silently. He nodded. Gradually the spasm passed and her mother sank back against the pillows, her small face deathly white. Emma took the chamber pot from her father and carried it through to the bucket in the scullery. She washed it out and brought it back in case it was needed again, then she added some small sticks to the fire and got it going. Her mother lay against the pillows, her eyes closed, but her breathing seemed very shallow.

'Has this happened before?' she asked softly. Her father wiped his brow.

'Aye, but never as bad as this; never so much blood,' he said on a note of despair.

'Should I go for Doctor Burns?'

'No, lassie.' Bert Greig shook his head. 'He said this might happen but there's nothing anyone can do. She — she's near the end, Emmie.' His voice broke. Emma shoved the kettle over the fire and brought the bowl her mother used to wash herself. She poured in some warm water then gently sponged her mother's face and hands and patted them dry. Bert watched, thankful she was here with him, calm and capable, gentle and loving.

'Will you pass me the cloth, lassie?' He wiped his own face and washed his hands before Emma carried the bowl away.

'I'll make you a cup of tea,' she offered. He didn't answer but Emma made it anyway. It had been her mother's cure for all situations. She poured them both a cup and then she sat on the opposite side of the hearth. Her heart ached with sadness but there were no words to express the way they both felt.

They had drunk the hot tea and Emma rose to take her father's empty cup.

'Emmie? Ye've come back.' Her mother's voice was little more than a whisper. She had opened her eyes but they had a dreamy, faraway look. 'You were always a good bairn.' Her pale lips lifted in a faint smile. 'Bert . . .' She reached for his hand and he clasped hers in both of his. Tears were running freely down his weathered cheeks.

Emma didn't know she was holding her breath until her father said quietly, 'She's gone.'

'Oh, Dad!' Emma flung herself to her knees beside him and hugged him tightly, whether for his comfort or her own she didn't know. He stroked her hair.

'Your mother is at peace now, lassie. No more suffering. You mustn't grieve.'

'I kn-know.'

'We must try to be glad, for her sake. I couldn't bear to see her go on suffering as she has these past weeks.'

Emma had lifted Peter for his early morning feed and she was thankful when he went back to sleep again. Both Meg and Jamie slept later than usual after the previous day's exertions. Joe looked sad but not surprised when he came downstairs.

'I must send a telegram to William,' Emma said.

'I'll send it for you,' Joe offered. 'What shall I put?'

'Just say "Mother died at four this morning, more later".'

'All right,' Joe nodded. 'I'll call and tell Julie. I'm sure she'll keep Meg and Jamie with her today. She said you could borrow the pram for Peter if you like. She's got it out and given it a wash and polish. Would you like her to keep him too?'

'No,' Bert Greig said before Emma had time to reply. 'I'll take him for a walk when he wakens. It will be something to do. I need to get out of the house for a bit. We'll walk away from the village and I'll call at Annie's and tell her.'

'All right, Dad, if you're sure,' Emma said. She realized he had never left the house, or her mother's side, since she arrived and she wondered how long before that. She saw the shock on Joe's face as he also guessed his father had probably not been out of the house for several weeks.

A telegram came for Emma just before midday. William sent his love and sympathy and said she must stay for the funeral. A letter was following. Sure enough the letter arrived with the traditional black edging the following morning. William could write a good letter when he set his mind to it and Emma was proud to let her father read his words of sympathy to him and the rest of her family. He said he had also written to Maggie by the same post asking her to bring butter, eggs, ham and lamb for the funeral tea and anything else she thought might be needed and he would send funds to pay for them. Much to his father's relief, Joe had offered to deal with the formalities of registering the death and making arrangements for the funeral so it was the following day before he walked up to Bonnybrae to tell the Sinclairs the news. He was surprised when he ran into Jim and he had already heard.

'We had a letter from William giving us the news,' Jim said. 'The postman brought it about an hour ago.'

'Oh I see. I'm sorry I couldn't come sooner,' Joe apologized.

'You would have plenty to do yesterday,' Jim said sympathetically.

'Aye. My father says I must tell Maggie, she will be welcome to come to the funeral if she can get away, but she has not to think of bringing food. It was kind of William to think of it. Emma and Julie are busy baking today and the children are with Annie. Everybody is doing their best to help but my father looks like a lost soul. He's going to feel it badly when Emma and the bairns go home — they will have to get back the day after the funeral.' James Sinclair had joined them in time to hear most of their conversation.

'The three of us will be at the funeral, Joe,' he said firmly. 'Maggie wants you to come into the kitchen for a cup of coffee. My wife has gone back to bed. She's having a bad day.' His mouth tightened. It had taken him years to realize that Mary Sinclair had always to be the centre of attention and when she was not, she invented some sort of ailment to gain sympathy. 'Maggie will want to bring something towards the funeral tea and we wouldn't take William's money for it so don't worry. I expect he wanted to help when he can't be here to give Emma his support.'

'I suppose so,' Joe said, 'but it was good of him to think of it and to write.' He followed Jim and his father into the Bonnybrae kitchen for a cup of coffee and one of Maggie's scones. She gave him her warm smile.

'Have the children recovered from their day by the sea?' she asked.

'They have, but I must be getting old,' Joe grinned. 'It tired me out too.'

'Mmm, and me,' Maggie confessed. 'You can take the eggs and some milk and a block of butter back with you, Joe, in case Emma needs it to bake.' She held up her hand when Joe would have protested. 'We want to help, don't we, Father?'

'Aye, I was telling him that.'

'Tell Emma I am cooking a ham to bring. We can slice it while the men are at the kirk yard. William suggested lamb but cold mutton is not so appetising.'

'No, and we have a shelf full of pickles and chutneys,' Joe said. 'Emma says that makes the meat go further. I ordered a large cheese from the grocer so with fresh bread and scones, as well as Emma's fruit loaf and apple pie and Julie's sponges and gingerbread, there should be plenty.'

'Yes, I'm sure Emma is a good provider,' Maggie agreed. 'I may not get a chance to mention it but I'll bring the pony and trap to take Emma and the children to the station the next morning. Will you tell her?'

'I will and I know she'll be very grateful.'

'Why don't you suggest your father goes back to Yorkshire with Emma and the bairns on the train?' James Sinclair said. 'He's nursed your mother constantly these past few months. They were always close friends when we were at school and I don't think either of them ever looked at another sweetheart. He's bound to miss her terribly. A change of scenery might help him come to terms with his loss. Tell him I'd like to hear all about William and what he's doing and where he lives. It might encourage him. I'm sure Emma would be pleased to have his company for a while.'

'Aye, if I put it like that and tell him Emma needs him he might agree,' Joe said, brightening. 'Otherwise, knowing Father he'll think he shouldn't leave me on my own, but I shall have to get back to work and we have a canteen for workers since last year so I get a good dinner there at midday. Yes, I'll do my best to persuade him.'

All the children were naturally subdued and they were overawed by the number who came to the cottage to hear the minister say his prayers over their grandmother's coffin, then they watched as it was carried down the garden path and along to the kirk yard with all the men following. The women did their best to dry their tears and get on with preparing a meal for the mourners who returned to the house.

'I think I should take all the bairns with me to our house,' Annie offered. 'It will leave more room here and I shall be more use than I am at serving teas. Shall I take wee Peter in his pram, Emma?'

'That would be a big help, Annie. He was changed and fed just before the service so he should be all right until you're ready to bring them all back. It will be good for them to be away from here and play together.'

It was an exhausting day but Emma knew her mother would have been astonished at the number of people who came to say a last farewell to her and she would have been proud of the family, providing a good tea for them all. Several of them lingered in little groups, talking in the garden or the older women sitting reminiscing by the fire. The only sour moment had been Aunt Vera, clinging to Uncle Derek's arm as though she was in deepest mourning but Emma had stayed with her aunt and uncle near Glasgow when she was unmarried and expecting Jamie, and she knew how selfish and resentful Vera was. Any show of grief was just a pretence. Vera had wanted to stay overnight but Richard had been firm about telling her there was no room and Emma and the children were leaving the morning after the funeral, and would have no time to be washing extra bedding. Emma breathed a sigh of relief. She knew she could never forget her aunt's mean and spiteful nature or her idleness. Worse, she would never forgive her for her callous neglect when Jamie was born and might have died had it not been for the wife of her uncle's employer. She avoided her as far as possible and was glad she had to leave early to catch the train back to Glasgow.

She had been surprised at James Sinclair's suggestion that her father should accompany them back to Yorkshire and she wondered why she had not thought of it herself. He was so obviously lost without her mother; he would feel even worse when she and the children returned to Yorkshire and Joe was at work all day.

'If I get a fortnight back at work I can organize my schedule, then I could come down for a weekend so we can travel back together,' Joe suggested. That seemed to reassure her father about the long train journey, but Emma guessed it was Meg and Jamie's eager response that persuaded him.

'Oh please come with us, Granddad!' Meg pleaded. 'I could show you the baby calves and where we go to school and you will see Allan and John and little Marie. She's just learned to walk and she keeps falling over.'

'I'll show you the puppies if you come, Granddad,' Jamie said. 'We could go for a walk to the common. The gypsies will have come back and you can meet Garridan. He's got a pretty wife and a little brown baby and he knows how to do all sorts of things, like catching rabbits and making wooden toys.'

Bert looked down into the honest, innocent young faces and admitted he would like to see where they lived and all the things they could show him.

'Will it be all right with William, lassie?' he asked diffidently.

'Of course it will, Dad.' Emma hugged him warmly and for a moment he clung to her, finding comfort in the warmth and contact. Emma hastily packed his clothes and their own ready for an early start.

As they got nearer to Wakefield, Emma wondered what William would think when he saw her father had come to visit. There had been no time to tell him their plans since she had written to tell him the time of the train on which they would be returning the day after the funeral. He had replied by return to say he would send the pony and trap to meet them at Silverwood Junction because he couldn't get to Wakefield in time. She knew he would be busy with the afternoon milking, so she understood. He had told her how much he was missing her. In the ten years since they married, they had never spent a night apart from each other.

Emma need not have worried about her husband's reaction. He was surprised to see Bert Greig but his smile was instant and warm as he took his father-in-law's hand in his firm grasp.

'You're very welcome,' he said, shaking Bert's hand. 'It's good to know that one member of our family is not too ashamed to visit us,' he said. Although he was smiling he couldn't quite hide the twinge of hurt and bitterness he had felt since his own family had despatched him to Yorkshire like an unwanted parcel.

'Eh laddie,' Bert Greig said warmly, sensitive as always to the feelings of others. 'We're none of us ashamed of you. We have no cause. As a matter of fact I know your father wished he was free to visit you. It was his suggestion that I should come and that I tell him all about your home and family and the farm when I return.'

'That's true, William,' Emma said quietly. 'I wished I'd thought of it myself. Joe is coming for a weekend in about a fortnight so he can travel back with Father.'

'You Greigs always were a close family,' William said with a reminiscent smile. 'I remember Emma's brothers always walked back with her to Bonnybrae after her Sunday off.'

'Your own family are just as close, and as loyal to ye as ever, laddie,' Bert said quietly. 'Except your mother maybe,' he added honestly, wondering if Jamie would tell his father about his meeting with his Grandmother Sinclair.

'I'll have to take your word for that,' William said with a wry smile.

'I promise ye 'tis true,' Bert assured him earnestly. 'Maggie has been an angel in disguise. She often dropped in to see my Lizzie if she was in the village, but when she took ill Maggie came as often as she could and she always brought some of her baking, or some cooked meat. She's a wonderful woman.'

'Aye, Maggie always had a good heart,' William agreed, 'and she writes to us every week, but she rarely mentions Mother.'

'Your father and Jim came to the funeral with Maggie,' Bert said. James Sinclair had admitted he couldn't fathom his wife's bitter, unforgiving nature and he'd given up trying, but it wouldn't do any good to tell William that.

When William drew the pony and trap into the farmyard, Bert Grieg stared.

'You said in your letters that the house was big, Emma, but I never imagined it would be as big as this. I wondered if I'd need to sleep in the barn,' he added, only half joking.

'Oh no. We keep a spare bedroom. Mrs Blackford sometimes stays and sleeps in it but while we have been away she will have been sleeping in Meg's bed to keep an eye on wee Marie.' She turned to William. 'Have the children been good while I have been away, and has the work gone all right?'

'The bairns have been very good, or so Maisie and Polly tell me but we have all missed you, Emmie. Even the cows I reckon. We've a gallon less milk and we have run out of butter.'

'Never mind,' Emma smiled. 'It's nice to be missed. We'll set some cream in the creaming pans tonight and tomorrow then I'll be able to make more butter.'

'Polly is hoping you would be able to churn tomorrow. She set milk in the creaming pans last night and skimmed the cream today. There will be more by tomorrow. I meant it when I said we had missed you terribly, Emmie, but if you're very tired tomorrow you must rest. We can survive on bread and dripping until you recover.'

'I'm sure I shall be fine after a good sleep,' Emma assured him. 'It's strange but even Peter has been good while we have been away and while we were travelling on the train. I hope he will keep it up now we're home.'

Bert listened to their chatter. He was pleased Emma and William seemed to be happy together in spite of being forced into married life, but his own heart was heavy, if it was possible for an empty heart to feel like a dead weight on his chest. Even here, where everything was new and different there was a gap in his life without his beloved Lizzie. How glad she would have been if she could have been with him now and seen Emma and William together in their home, happy with their growing family.

Since the first day they arrived at Moorend, with Jamie as a baby, Polly and Cliff Barnes had shared their home as live-in workers. Emma and William had fallen into a habit of keeping their personal conversations until they went to bed where they could discuss things in private. As soon as they were alone that evening William took her in his arms and kissed her tenderly, then gently took the pins from her hair so that he could run his fingers through the soft shining tresses. He had always loved to see it falling over her shoulders. He had many questions to ask about their families.

'I can feel your tension, dearest Emmie,' he said softly. 'Let's get into bed where we shall be warm and you can tell me everything. I am so thankful you got there in time to see your mother and talk to her.'

'Oh so am I, William, so am I,' Emma said fervently. 'She was so very happy to see me, and the children too.' Her voice grew husky with emotion and William drew her closer.

'Tell me what happened, Emmie.' She explained about her mother's illness.

'She had grown so thin and weak. I shall always be grateful to Maggie and Julie for telling me. I-I had never seen a dead person before. I'm so glad I was there with my father though, but then . . . then I felt I had to blank it all out so that I could be strong for him and for Joe, although . . .' She paused and turned into the circle of his arm to watch his face in the candlelight. 'It's strange, but Joe seemed to find comfort in Maggie's company.'

'Maggie's? My sister Maggie?'

'Yes. My father says she's been really good at calling to see them ever since we left Scotland. He says she never came empty handed, especially this past year when Mother's health began to fail.'

'Maggie always had a kind heart,' William reflected. 'I wonder what my mother thought to that.'

'I doubt if she would know. Apparently she suffered an attack of apoplexy some time ago. She walks with a stick now and it seems she mainly spends her day beside the fire in her room.' Emma was silent, her face troubled as she wondered whether she should tell William how she had greeted Jamie.

'What's the matter, Emmie? Did you see my mother? Did she treat you badly?" His arm tightened.

'I didn't see her, b-but your father and Jim wanted to see Jamie and Meg. Joe went with them and Maggie in the trap, then Joe walked them back.'

'So what's troubling you? You might as well tell me, Emmie, my love.'

'Well, please promise you will not get angry or upset.'

'I can guess this has something to do with my mother. Was she stirring up trouble with innocent bairns?'

'She — she called Jamie a — a bastard.' Emma went on hurriedly. 'Maggie says she behaves immaturely sometimes since she's been ill so maybe she didn't mean to call him that.'

'Oh, she would mean it all right,' William said bitterly.

'He doesn't really understand what it means, just that you have told him it's a bad word and he's not to use it. B-but . . .' Emma's eyes filled with tears. 'She told him his name is Greig and he's not a Sinclair. He didn't know what she was talking about. But William, he — he will one day. It says Greig on his birth certificate.'

'Hell! I never thought of that. How can a woman be so bitter she takes it out on her own grandchild?'

'You promised you wouldn't be angry,' Emma pleaded. His mouth twisted in a wry smile.

'I don't think I promised because I guessed it was something to do with my mother. I thought you might be worrying about your father. Are you?'

'No, not really. In fact I'm glad he has come to see where we live and get to know our other children. It was your father's idea that he should come back with us. It was all a last minute decision and a bit of a rush to pack our clothes. Your father and Jim and Maggie all came to the funeral and your father is really sorry your mother treated Jamie and Meg the way she did. He apologised to me, and to my father. I think they may renew their old friendship. It will be good for both of them.'

'I'm amazed. Father always seemed to bend over backwards to avoid upsetting my mother. I can't imagine she will be pleased at being left behind.'

'I don't think she knows what's going on. I had no idea that Joe and Maggie had become so friendly.'

'Well that's good in my opinion,' William said firmly. 'Everybody needs friends and Maggie has made too many sacrifices to please our mother. As soon as she saw her chatting to any of the young men after the kirk, or heard of her seeing any of them more than once, she made all sorts of ridiculous excuses or accusations why none of them were suitable as friends.'

'Mmm, well I'm wondering if there's more than friendship between Joe and Maggie.'

'Really? I would never have believed they would get to know each other well enough. Are you sure you're not just being romantic, Emmie?'

'I don't think so.' She told him about Joe and Maggie taking the children to the seaside for the day and how much they had all enjoyed it.

'I suppose people are never too old for love,' William mused. 'The sad thing is Maggie will be too old to have children and she would have been a wonderful mother. I would be pleased for both of them though, especially if they can share the same happiness as we have. I don't know what would happen at Bonnybrae if they wanted to get married. My father and Jim would miss Maggie terribly but there would be hell to pay with Mother. She would never speak to them again if she's the way she is with us. She has always treated Maggie differently somehow.'

On Sunday, Emma was pleased when her father said he would like to accompany them to church. 'The service is quite different to our kirk back home,' she said, 'but we have a prayer book to follow and it gives all the responses. We'll sit near the back until you see what I mean. The old oak pews are so high people can barely see anyone else when we're all kneeling.'

'It sounds more complicated than the service in our ain wee kirk but I'd like to go the first Sunday . . .' Emma nodded in understanding, knowing he was thinking of her mother. 'We didn't get to the kirk at all these past months but Julie's father called in nearly every week and said a prayer with us and he gave us Holy Communion the week before you came. His visits seemed to comfort your mother.'

'I'm sure they would. She never liked to miss the kirk.'

Although Silverbeck village church was not the main one for the parish it was usually well attended by the local people; Lord Hanley attended once a month with his family instead of going to the parish church, as was their habit. After the service the congregation stood and waited while the vicar and the choirboys filed up the aisle, followed by Lord Hanley and family and the rest of the church dignitaries. Emma thought she saw a look of surprise on Mr Rowbottom's face as he caught sight of her. She didn't know that Thora Wilkins had seen her sitting on the train for Scotland with two of the children and the baby, but without her husband. She had quickly spread the rumour that Sinclair's wife had got fed up with milking cows and bearing children. She had run away back to Scotland and left him. She had lost no time in repeating her story to Mr Rowbottom when he called at Mountcliffe to discuss the installation of a water closet. He had already been to Moorend on the same business. He knew William was busy ploughing and unavailable to discuss matters but it was unusual not to see anything of Emma.

Emma was surprised to find Mr Rowbottom and his wife waiting to greet them as they left the church. As they approached he saw that William and the old man at his side were both wearing black ties and Emma was in a black dress and coat with black hat and gloves.

'We missed you at church, Mrs Sinclair. William . . .' Although his voice did not rise in question, his eyebrows did.

'Emma was away in Scotland visiting her mother,' William said gravely. 'She was very ill. Fortunately Emma was in time to spend a little time with her before she died. This is my father-in-law, Mr Bert Greig. He is spending a couple of weeks with us.' The two men shook hands.

'I am so sorry for your loss, Mr Greig, but I am pleased to meet you.' Bert Greig responded quietly, surprised and pleased that the land agent should bother to greet his daughter and son-in-law.

'You can walk on with the children, Polly,' Emma said, seeing her two younger sons fidgeting and Meg trying to keep them quiet.

'I'm sure they feel they have been good long enough after sitting through the service,' Mrs Rowbottom smiled. 'I always think the vicar makes the sermon a bit longer when he knows Lord Hanley will be here.'

'You're right, Mrs Rowbottom,' William said. 'I hadn't thought of it before.'

'We'll not keep you,' Mr Rowbottom said, 'but I would like to say, Mr Greig, you have every reason to be proud of your daughter, and your son-in-law. They have worked extremely hard ever since they took over the tenancy of Moorend. You would not have recognized the house, or the farmyard, if you had seen it when they arrived. Many a young woman would have run back to her family in tears, but I think William knows he's a lucky man.' William caught Emma's eye and winked. He often teased her about Mr Rowbottom admiring her and singing her praises.

'I'm glad to hear you say so, Mr Rowbottom,' Bert Greig said. 'It's a splendid house now. Emma has always been a hard worker. My only regret is I didn't think to travel so far while my wife was alive. She would have loved to see them so happy and the bairns all healthy and thriving.'

'It is easy to know what we should have done with hindsight,' Mrs Rowbottom said gently, 'but I'm sure Emma and William are very glad you have come to visit now. The children will be enjoying having their grandfather to stay.'

'They certainly are,' Emma said, 'but he gets no peace. If they're not taking him to see the puppies, it's the calves, or hunting for bird nests.'

'Jamie has already taken him to see the gypsies,' William said. He didn't add they had returned with a hare for the pot, which Garridan had insisted on giving them, nor did he voice his concerns about Jamie's increasing restlessness and his eagerness to spend time with the gypsies as soon as they returned. He loved to hear about their travels.

Emma felt the past two weeks had passed far too quickly when Joe sent word he would be arriving as he had promised. He came on the late train on Friday after he finished work for the day. William met him at Wakefield station and explained they needed to catch the local train to Silverbeck.

'I left the pony and trap there but it was too far to drive to Wakefield and straight back home again. Dolly, the pony, is getting old. We have lamps for the trap for short journeys but we don't venture far in the dark.'

'I'm very grateful you could meet me,' Joe said. 'It's not easy seeing where we are when it's dark. I would probably have got the wrong train and ended up miles away.'

'I'm glad to have a chance to talk to you, Joe. We hardly knew each other back home but we've heard a lot about you from Jamie and Meg so I don't think they'll give you much time alone.'

'They're grand bairns,' Joe said warmly. 'Maggie and I really enjoyed taking them to see the sea.'

'Emma tells me you and Maggie have become great friends?'

'We have.' Joe hesitated, then went on, 'Maggie is a fine person. She is as genuine as they come. I never thought I would ever meet any woman I would want to share every day of my life with. I never get tired of Maggie's company. She says she feels the same but we both know there are too many obstacles for us to get married and set up house together.' He sighed heavily.

'You mean my mother? She has always been extraordinarily possessive where Maggie is concerned. I don't suppose Maggie will leave her now if she is dependent on her.'

'No, I couldn't ask her to do that. We both treasure whatever time we manage to spend together. Maggie gets exasperated with her mother's unreasonable demands but the old lady needs a lot of help since the apoplexy. I wouldn't feel too happy about leaving my own father on his own now either, though I know he would never stand in my way if I wanted to set up home with Maggie. Julie and Davy are very good at looking in on him. He doesn't realize we know he has heart trouble, but Doctor Burns admitted he has warned him to take things easy. Apparently digging, bending, or lifting could bring on a heart attack, but he has always loved his garden. It's his pride and joy.'

'I see,' William said thoughtfully. 'That may be why he gets so tired by evening. We thought it was the children asking him to do too much, especially after the months of stress and his grief at losing your mother.'

'That hasna helped,' Joe agreed. 'Emma doesn't know about Doctor Burns' warning. Promise me you will not tell her? The reason I suggested coming was so he wouldn't be anxious about the return journey on his own.'

'Are you sure it's the right thing to do, keeping it from Emmie?'

'We all agreed. She would only worry. I am glad your father suggested he should come and visit you all. His visit might be a comfort to her later.'

'We have all enjoyed having him to stay,' William said sincerely.

CHAPTER SIX

The weekend passed all too quickly. It was William who accompanied Joe and his father to Wakefield and saw them on the train. He knew Emma would be upset when they had to say goodbye and she hated anyone to see her tears, especially in public.

The train was fairly busy for the first part of the journey and Bert Grieg sat silently in his corner seat gazing out of the window, apparently deep in thought. All but one of the other passengers had left their carriage and there were lambs in many of the fields as they passed through the Yorkshire Dales.

'Young Jamie longs for his father to get some breeding ewes so they can have lambs,' Bert said, breaking the silence. 'He's not keen on the cows like Emmie and William, but he's already teaching his dog how to round up the sheep William takes on for winter grazing.'

'I expect he takes after his father in that respect at least,' Joe said. 'Maggie often talks about William training the collie dogs to herd the sheep at Bonnybrae. I think he would like some ewes if they had more land. Did you enjoy your visit, Father?'

'Aye, laddie, I'm glad I've been. My only regret is that I didna take your mother to visit while she was well enough.

She would have been so pleased to see the bairns and see for herself how well Emma and William are getting on. It's true they work hard but they're making a place to be proud of and they seem satisfied with their lot.'

'They must have worked very hard, I reckon,' Joe agreed. 'William told me what a mess everything was when they first arrived. He said he couldn't have blamed Emma if she had run away home at the sight of the filthy house and he'll always be grateful for the way she stuck in and supported him. He said every drawer and cupboard was stuffed with everything from clothes to pots, even cracked ones. He reckoned the previous tenant never cleared anything out, and it was the same outside with old tools and machines.'

'Aye, but they have salvaged some good stuff. I understand now why Emma never had time to come home for a visit but I'm truly thankful she arrived before your mother died.'

'Yes, seeing Emma and the bairns cheered her wonderfully. Emma is even more glad she arrived in time.'

'I can understand that, but I'd like ye to remember it's different in my case, Joe. I've seen Emma and her bairnies now. I've spent time with them; I know they're well and content. I don't ask for more. So I want you to promise, when my time comes, you willna tell Emmie until after my funeral.'

'Och, Father . . .'

'No, no, laddie. Promise me ye'll do as I ask, and make Julie and Maggie understand it's what I want. Emma and William have a lot of work to do every day. I don't want her leaving William again, or spending money to come to a funeral when I can't enjoy her company. I've had a grand fortnight with my wee lassie. I shall treasure that memory.' He was silent for a few moments then he seemed to make up his mind. 'Doctor Burns told me my heart is not as good as it ought to be. If he's right, and if the good Lord is kind to me, I'll not have to suffer like your mother.'

'What has Doctor Burns been telling you, Father?' Joe asked. He didn't feign surprise, but neither did he admit he already knew the doctor's opinion.

'Och, he only said I should take things easier, but you know laddie, it's not my style to sit around and worry about my health. I might have to take a bit more time to dig my garden or tend my plants but if the Lord sees fit to take me while I'm doing it, then what better place to be?' Joe opened his mouth to speak but Bert held up a hand. 'I've always enjoyed my garden. I know ye're willing to help, laddie, but I don't want any of you taking it over from me, and neither do I want you grieving, or feeling regrets.'

'I see . . .' Joe said slowly. 'I admit I can't see you being content to sit by the fire all day, but it would be no bother to me to dig over the garden and at least do the heavier work.' Bert's lined face crinkled in a smile but he shook his head.

'I'll let ye know when I want ye digging my garden, and I'm not saying I might not be glad of your help some day. All right, son?'

'If you say so,' Joe agreed wryly, smiling, knowing how fiercely independent both his parents had always been. They were both silent for a while but when the remaining passenger left them with the carriage to themselves, Bert began to talk again.

'Maggie Sinclair is a fine woman. I can see she thinks a lot o' ye, Joe, and I reckon ye feel the same about her. Don't miss your chance o' happiness lad. I don't want ye to consider me if the pair of ye get an opportunity to set up house together. I'm well blessed with all of you and Julie and Davy would make sure I was all right.'

Joe looked his father in the eye, then sighed. 'It is true I love Maggie and I long to make her my wife but you're not the one holding us back, Father. Maggie would never see you want for anything either. She and Julie are a lot alike, but I do understand your life can never be truly happy without Mother.'

'Ye're right there, laddie.' Bert sighed heavily. 'I'm not getting morbid ye understand, but half of me seems to have gone already and I'm content to go when my time comes.'

'I understand, Father. I can't see me leaving you on your own, though. Maggie cares deeply about her family, although

I do believe the old woman has overplayed her demands. Jim and Mr Sinclair are loyal but even they have been driven to criticise recently. Maggie is dedicated but her patience is being sorely tried. Mrs Sinclair keeps telling her she has made a lot of sacrifices for her benefit so it is her duty to care for her in her old age.'

'She always had a high opinion of herself did Mary Bowran, but she has no right to expect Maggie to be the only daughter to care for her, not unless . . .' he broke off, frowning. Then he seemed to give a mental shake and shrugged. 'The old woman canna live forever. Your turn will come, Joe.'

'What were you going to say, Father? Unless what? Did you know Mrs Sinclair when you were young?'

'Not like we knew James Her father owned a coal mine and she was his only bairn. It was said her mother died when she was young. Her father employed a woman to look after her. When she was old enough he sent her to school in Edinburgh. They used to live in a big house near Cumnock, or so she said. Her father sold the mine and his house. There were rumours he had lost part of his fortune after an accident but I couldna say about that. We only knew the Bowrans after Mary's father bought one of the big houses nearer to Stavondale.'

'Stavondale Tower? You mean they lived near Sir Reginald Capel of Stavondale, the Sinclairs' landlord?'

'Aye, he's the only Baronet Capel around here that I know of.' Bert smiled reminiscently. 'Sir Reginald was just Mr Capel the Younger then, though, as his son is now. He would be about a couple of years older than James Sinclair and me and our wee gang. He was a bit of a rebel at that time though. There was nothing snooty or aristocratic about him, not like the present young Mr Capel, they say.'

'I've heard Jim Sinclair say the young laird is not easy to deal with but while Sir Reginald is still alive, he can't make too many changes to the tenancies without his father's approval. Did you meet him in his younger days then, Father?' Joe asked curiously.

'Och aye. He was a great one for the dancing. I dinna think his father would have approved if he'd known half the tricks he got up to. Mary Bowran, as she was then, set her cap at him. So did some of the other lassies but Mary was the prettiest and she was better educated than the rest of us. Her father bought her all the gowns she wanted. At least he did until the money began to run out. It was said Mr Bowran had made some bad investments but we didn't understand such things. She never had any time for the likes o' your mother and me but we didna care. We had each other. I never looked at any other lass than your mother, but most of the other lads fancied Mary Bowran, even though she could be a snooty wee madam. She could have had her pick o' nearly any of the farmers' sons in those days, including James Sinclair, but she set her heart on the young Mr Capel, as Sir Reginald was then. He led her on shamefully too, yet he must have known his parents expected him to marry the daughter of a landowner from Dumfriesshire. The wedding was all arranged before Mary Bowran learned of his intentions — or at least before she really believed he intended to marry somebody else. James Sinclair had been one of her admirers for some time, so I suppose it shouldn't have been a surprise when they married so soon after the young laird's betrothal was announced. James's father was the biggest tenant on the estate but we all knew she had hoped to be the future Lady Capel.' Joe had never heard his father talk so much about the past and he was reluctant to interrupt.

After a while Bert went on, frowning a little. Joe assumed it was the effort of remembering. 'We didna see much o' James after that. I expect he was occupied looking after his family. They had young Maggie well before the year was up. Mary favoured the kirk, and later the school, over the other side of Bonnybrae in East Lowry, so they didn't come to Locheagle much. We all thought she wanted to keep him away from the likes of us, the friends he had been with at school and while he was growing into a man and sowing his wild oats.' Bert fell silent again. There was no point in resurrecting old rumours after so long, and they had only ever been rumours. Joe loved Maggie Sinclair and she was a fine woman; that was all that mattered.

Although Joe had only been away for a weekend, Maggie had missed him dreadfully. Her mother had been even more difficult and demanding than usual and Maggie realized how much she had come to depend on Joe's cheerful company to help her cope with the increasing burden.

'Mother has been so confused — I don't understand what she's talking about,' she said when she and Joe met on the Tuesday evening after his return. She had driven down to Locheagle with her father because he wanted to hear how Bert Greig had got on visiting Emma and William. Joe and Maggie left the two older men together by the fire and went for a walk in the nearby woods.

'I do understand how tied you feel,' Joe said, 'but I wish I could have taken you with me. Even such a short break would have done you good. Emma and William would have been delighted to see you.'

'Yes, I know.' Maggie sighed heavily. 'I would love to have gone with you, Joe. I don't know how I survived before I knew you.'

'I don't suppose your mother needed so much care then. We all grow old.'

'Mother was never strong after William was born. I know she lost a lot of blood and nearly died, but she recovered. She used to work hard when we were all young. She believes William and Emma brought disgrace to Bonnybrae so she has not been to the kirk since then and she has become . . . almost vicious. It was Mother who insisted William must leave the area because he had caused a scandal. She even objected when Father gave him money, although William had earned it. Father said if his son had to leave home he would not see him penniless. She resented that. As far as I know it was the nearest my parents ever came to a quarrel. None of the boys were paid wages but they all knew Father would help them rent a farm and buy stock when they were of an age to set up on their own. He intended to do the same for William but he wasn't ready to do it so soon, or so urgently.' Joe stopped walking along the woodland path and led Maggie towards a sturdy old oak tree. He leaned back against the trunk and drew her against him, smoothing back her thick, wavy hair with gentle fingers.

'I reckon your father will be proud of William, aye and Emmie. They're working hard and making a good job of farming. Nobody would believe the farm had been derelict when they went there.' He lowered his head and sought her mouth. Maggie responded with all the eagerness of a young girl. She had been surprisingly shy the first time Joe had taken her in his arms and kissed her. It had surprised then delighted him to find he was the first man to awaken the latent desire in her. Now they were completely at ease together, each knowing their love was reciprocated as they kissed and held each other close. Neither of them talked of their future. Maggie had a strong sense of duty and Joe understood she would not leave Bonnybrae while her mother needed her, however difficult she became. At the same time Maggie knew Joe was too proud and independent to move into Bonnybrae.

'I long for us to be together all the time, night and day,' she said softly, her lips just a breath away from Joe's. His arms tightened and he held her even closer against the length of his body.

'You know it is what I want too, Maggie, my love.' He gave a little sigh. 'My mother always said God had a way of working things out, but sometimes I wonder if there is a solution for us.'

One Saturday morning Joe rose very early, ignoring his father's claim that he would do his own digging. They always grew a fair sized patch of early potatoes and by the time Bert Greig came down for breakfast, Joe had the area well turned over with not a weed to be seen. He set about making the drills ready for the manure. He knew his father was both relieved and pleased when he came into the garden and exclaimed in surprise.

'I thought ye were still in bed, Joe, and here ye've done a day's work already.' He moved to the end of the plot and eyed the drills. 'Eh laddie, they're as straight and true as any I ever made myself.'

'I'm glad you approve.' Joe grinned happily. He had not been too sure how his father would react. 'I wanted to get the ground ready. Mr Sinclair is coming down early this afternoon with the horse and cart. He's bringing us a load of good muck.'

'Is he? How much does he want for it?'

'I didn't ask. He offered to bring it. I think he enjoys coming down to Locheagle for a bit of peace and a good natter about old times.'

'Aye, we always got on well when we were laddies and I enjoy his talk now your mother isna here. Julie said she would be round later with the bairns. She's bringing some scones and a cake. I shall be able to offer James some tea.'

As things turned out it was Jim who drove down to Locheagle to bring the load of manure. 'Father says he's sorry he couldna come for a chat, Mr Greig. Mother has had a turn for the worse. Maggie was up with her all night. Father has sent her to bed for an hour or two so he's sitting with Mother himself. She keeps trying to get out of bed and talking a lot of nonsense as far as I can gather. She really upsets Maggie when she starts to shout. The doctor says it's part of her illness. He left some medicine to try and calm her and let her sleep.'

When Jim returned in time for the milking, his father emerged from the downstairs bedroom.

'I don't know what the doctor gave your mother, she's slept peacefully all afternoon but I shall need to waken Maggie before we go out to the byre.'

'No need, Father,' Maggie said, coming into the kitchen. 'I feel better for a rest and I looked in on Mother. She's still asleep so I will get on with preparing an evening meal until she wakens.'

Later, when Mary Sinclair wakened, Maggie took her in a small dish of egg custard, well sprinkled with nutmeg.

It was one of her mother's favourites and easily digested, but she had no appetite and only ate a few mouthfuls before she sank back against her pillows, half sleeping, yet murmuring names unknown to Maggie.

'She hasna eaten enough to keep a mouse alive,' Maggie said when she brought the tray back through to the kitchen. She began to clear away and wash up after their meal. Jim went out to finish a few jobs before the spring day faded.

'It's no good worrying, lassie,' James Sinclair said, putting a comforting arm around Maggie's shoulders. 'The doctor says her life is drawing to a close and we must let her die in peace. He left some more medicine but he said we must only give it to her if she becomes delirious or violent again and tries to get out of bed. I'll sit in her room for a while. Jim brought a newspaper for me to read.' Maggie nodded and went on tidying up the kitchen and preparing as much as she could for the following day. She would have to ask Mrs Edgar to work some extra hours if her mother was as bad again tonight.

When she went through to the bedroom, she found her father reading his newspaper beside the fire while her mother lay propped against her pillows with her eyes closed, but as soon as she heard the latch of the door opening she opened her eyes and held out a hand beckoning Maggie to come closer.

'Can I get you something, Mother? A cup of tea?'

'No, no.' She brushed the suggestion aside with a feeble hand. 'You have to understand. I tried to make amends and be a good Christian all my life.' Her voice sank to a whisper. 'But I couldn't confess my sin. I should have told him.' Maggie's heart sank. This was how her mother had begun during the night, talking nonsense then shouting in frustration when Maggie tried to soothe her. But her words had been slurred then, jumbling into one another, incomprehensible to Maggie. Now she was perfectly lucid and her eyes no longer held the wild desperation of the night. 'I tried to be a good wife. I made sure we both worked hard and did our duty, you as well as me. We earned your keep.' Her hands were twisting in agitation again. Maggie sat on the edge of the bed and took them in hers.

'We all know you went to church regularly when you could, Mother. God knows and He will forgive whatever sins you may have.'

'But I deceived . . .' Her voice began to rise. 'I should have told him before we married. I knew we had sinned. I panicked. Later . . . later I knew Reginald must be your father, Maggie, but I still couldna tell him. He's a good man. He deserved the truth . . .' Her voice petered into silence. She closed her eyes. Maggie still clasped her hands, holding them still, trying to give reassurance. She glanced up and was surprised to see her father had laid aside his newspaper and was leaning forward in his chair, his eyes alert, listening intently.

'She was talking nonsense like this last night,' Maggie told him wearily. 'Only I couldn't make out what she was saying most of the time. When I tried to hush her she began to shout and tried to get out of bed. Her speech is clear tonight but . . .'

'It's all right, lassie, I understand now why she's been so troubled.' To Maggie's surprise her father came and knelt at the other side of the bed. He took one of her mother's hands into his own warm, work roughened hands. He spoke in a low voice. 'She's thinking o' the past. I believe she knows her end is near. She needs to unburden herself so she can die in peace.' They sat silent for a while, one on each side of the bed. Her mother seemed to be sleeping and Maggie was reluctant to disturb her by moving. Eventually her eyelids lifted.

'Mary,' James Sinclair said her name and Maggie heard the note of urgency in his voice. 'Mary, look at me. It's James, your husband.'

'James?' Her voice was little more than a whisper.

'Aye, your husband, Mary. Listen to me. You have been a good wife . . .'

'I deceived you. I should have confessed when I knew for sure.'

'It was never a secret from me, Mary. I've known Sir Reginald was Maggie's father since the day she was born.'

'You knew? All these years?'

'I was content. I had the woman I wanted for my wife. We made our vows, remember. For better, for worse. Whoever had sired our bairn I could never wish for a better daughter than Maggie . . .' He looked up suddenly, remembering Maggie's presence. Her face was white, her eyes were wide with shock. She stared at them in disbelief. She jumped up from the bed.

'I don't believe it,' she said hoarsely.

'We'll talk about it later, lassie,' James said gently, almost apologetically. 'You get some rest. I'll stay with her tonight. I think she may find peace now.'

Maggie's throat worked convulsively but no words would come. She turned and left the room. Blindly she headed for the kitchen and bumped into her brother, Jim — only he wasn't her brother, was he? Not if her mother was really telling the truth.

'Maggie!' Jim steadied her, his hands on her shoulders, his face showing concern. 'What's wrong? Is it Mother? Has she? Has she . . . ?'

'N-no. Oh Jim, what am I to do? I can't believe it. I thought Mother was rambling, delirious . . .'

'Aye, you said she talked nonsense most of the night. Is she as bad again now the doctor's medicine has worn off?'

'F-Father says it's not nonsense. He says it's the truth. He thinks that's what has been troubling her for so long. He — he says he's not my father, Jim.' She drew back and looked up into his startled face.

'Och, you must have misunderstood, Maggie.' She shook her head and tears poured silently down her pale cheeks. Jim wiped them away awkwardly with the pad of his thumb. He'd never seen Maggie cry since she was a little girl. She had always been the happiest of the family with a quiet dignity and control all of her own.

'You've had a shock, Maggie, and you're exhausted. You go and get ready for bed. I'll make you a drink of hot milk and bring it up to you. I'll put a wee drop of brandy in it. It will help you sleep.' Jim had never been the least bit domesticated. Maggie summoned a wobbly smile.

'I'm n-not a starved orphan lamb . . .' she protested.

'If it's good for them it will be good for you. Now do as I say. I'll bring it up in a minute or two.' Maggie felt too drained and bewildered to protest further.

Jim had been exceedingly generous with the brandy, then added honey to camouflage the taste. He waited until Maggie had sipped it all then took the mug and bid her a gruff goodnight. Maggie didn't expect to sleep at all with so many thoughts churning in her head, but she was exhausted both mentally and physically. She couldn't believe it when she opened her eyes and looked at her clock. She should have been up and had the fire kindled and the kettle boiling an hour ago. She washed her face and hands in the cold water on her washstand and dressed hastily. She felt a little groggy and she guessed Jim had added more brandy than he should have.

In the kitchen the fire was already blazing merrily in the range and Mrs Edgar was stirring the porridge. She turned with a smile when Maggie entered.

'Jim came for Edgar and me. He said you were exhausted and he had dosed you with brandy to make you sleep. You were needing a good night's rest, lassie. Edgar and me were beginning to wonder how much longer you could carry on.'

'I-I'm fine now. Thank you for coming up so early, Mrs Edgar.' She rubbed her forehead. 'Maybe I'm a bit groggy. I'm not used to spirits.'

'Jim was right. It would do you good. I never thought Mistress Sinclair would become such a restless, demanding patient but your father says she had a peaceful night. Thank the Lord.'

'Yes. I will peep in and check on her.'

In the two days that followed, Mary Sinclair barely spoke or ate. She sipped a little tea or water when Maggie held the feeding cup to her dry lips but she had no appetite for food. She seemed content now to lie back against her pillows and sleep. James Sinclair stayed with her again during the night, relieving Maggie of her care, but there had been no opportunity for her to ask the questions teaming in her mind. The following morning James drew Jim aside when they had loaded the milk churns into the cart to take to the station.

'Your mother willna last much longer, Jim. I'd really like William to come for the funeral. Maybe he'll bring the wee fellow again.'

'Do you think he'll want to come after — well, Mother treated both him and Emma so harshly? If what Maggie says is true it makes no sense that Mother should have acted the way she did. Of all people, she should have had some understanding.'

'I think she dreaded the gossip starting all over again, we'll talk about that later. But Jim,' he laid a hand on his arm for a moment, 'I think I understand a little of your mother's reasoning for turning so bitter and I know now why she was so possessive with Maggie, why she expected her to stay here and to work so hard.' He shook his head sorrowfully. 'There was never any need. But it's time ye were on your way to the station, laddie. We can talk things over later.'

CHAPTER SEVEN

Jim sent a telegram to William to say their mother was barely conscious but their father longed to see him.

'It sounds as though they expect the funeral to be soon,' Emma said thoughtfully when he showed her the telegram. 'I can understand how much your father wants to see you, William. I think Jim has sent this so you will be prepared. If the weather holds you will finish drilling the last field today, you said?'

'I intend to finish and set Tom to harrow in the seed by nightfall, now that we have another pair of horses. But surely Emma, you don't expect me to attend my mother's funeral after the way she treated both of us?'

'You would be going to give support to your father and Jim and Maggie. I haven't heard from Maggie this week. She must be worn out with caring for your mother and keeping house, even though she says Mrs Edgar has been a gem at helping her.'

'Well I don't feel like going to the funeral of a woman who couldn't find it in her heart to forgive. It's not as though either of us committed murder,' William said stubbornly. 'I should feel a hypocrite and I can't leave you to manage on your own.'

'You would only be away two nights,' Emma said gently. 'We shall manage between us, Tom and Polly and me. I know Cliff can't be relied on but young Billy is shaping up well, don't you think? I'm sure he and Meg could feed the calves and he could feed the bullocks in the foldyard.'

'It sounds as though you have it all planned, Emmie.'

'Well, Maggie has warned us how ill your mother is in her last few letters. Your father was so good to me when we married, buying material for new dresses for me and for Maggie, and he came to the wedding. He was so pleased to see Jamie when I took him to Scotland. Perhaps you could take him with you. Children have a way of easing awkward situations.'

'We'll see. Now I'd better get on with drilling the last field of oats.'

Late the following afternoon, a boy from the village came to Moorend and handed Emma another telegram. As she had expected, it confirmed that Mary Sinclair had died and gave the funeral arrangements. It ended, '*MAGGIE DEEPLY DISTRESSED ABOUT THINGS. PLEASE COME. JIM.*'

Reluctantly, William made plans to go to Bonnybrae. Jamie overheard his mother suggesting he should accompany his father and rushed in from the scullery.

'Oh yes, please can I come with you, Father? I didn't like the old woman who looked like a witch but . . .'

'Hush, Jamie!' Emma admonished. 'Your Grandma Sinclair has died.'

'I know. I would be able to see Granddad and his dogs and Uncle Jim. Would I be able to see Granddad Greig and Uncle Joe?' He watched his mother and father exchange glances. His father raised his eyebrows and shrugged.

'If you really think I should take the rascal then I will,' William said, 'although he ought to stay at home and help you like Meg will be doing.'

'Oh I don't mind. I like helping Mam and Polly,' Meg said quickly. 'Anyway,' she grinned at her brother, 'even Mam says Jamie is not very good at milking.'

'All the more reason for him to practise then,' William muttered. 'Oh all right then, I'll take him.' Later, when they were alone he said to Emma, 'I'll send a telegram to let them know. We shall have to stay at Bonnybrae. It will be a wonder if Mother doesn't rise up from her coffin at the thought of me staying under the same roof. She wouldn't let me stay when we were married. I had to stay with Beth.'

'Never mind, everything went well without her cooperation,' Emma soothed. 'It sounds as though Maggie has taken things very badly if Jim thinks she needs you.'

After the funeral, when the mourners had left and only Jim and Maggie remained with their father, William knew Emma had been right to send Jamie. Both Jim and his father seemed eager for the boy's company and Jamie went willingly to the byre with his Uncle Jim to help with the milking.

'Don't be in such a hurry, laddie,' Jim teased gently. 'It's not a race. Some cows let their milk flow more quickly than others but it's important that you should get the last drop out at each milking, otherwise they might get a disease called mastitis and then the cow might even lose that quarter of her udder altogether.'

'Mother never explained all that,' Jamie said.

'Sitting on a milking stool listening to the thrum of the milk in the pail can be very welcome after a hard day behind the plough, or after shearing sheep all day. There's many a worse job,' Jim assured him. 'Maybe you'll be able to travel on the train on your own when you're a bit older. You could come for your holidays now that — well, now that your grandmother is no longer with us.'

'Mam says we shouldn't speak badly of dead people but that old woman didn't like me.'

'She didn't really know you, laddie, and after her apoplexy she said many strange things. Anyway, you know both your grandfathers want to see you as often as they can and so do I, and your Aunt Maggie and Uncle Joe.' Jim was unaware of the seed he was planting in his nephew's mind in his effort to offer reassurance and compensate for the bitter way his mother had greeted the boy.

William had been dismayed when he first saw Maggie. She was thinner than he recalled and her face looked strained and colourless. When Jamie had gone to bed, William turned to his elder brother. 'Maggie doesn't look well. What was the other matter you said had distressed her?' He was aware of his father carefully folding his paper and laying it aside before he came to join them round the fire. Maggie was still in the scullery with Mrs Edgar, washing dishes and putting things away after the funeral tea.

'She has had a shock,' James Sinclair said. 'I have always loved her as my own daughter but I knew when she was born I was not the man who sired her.'

'What!' William exclaimed. 'You canna mean . . . you can't be saying . . . surely you can't mean Mother . . . ? She could never have treated Emma so harshly if she committed the same sin as we did!'

'It takes a lot of understanding to know how another person's mind works.' His father sighed heavily and William noticed the lines that etched his face. 'I admit I couldn't believe she had treated Emma so harshly and without even consulting me. Neither did I realize what was in her mind when she became hysterical after you said you were the father. She was adamant I must send you away to Yorkshire. I know now she thought the gossip and the old rumours would start all over again.'

'What old rumours?' William asked, his face grim.

'There were rumours when we were married.' His father sighed again. 'I always knew your mother was the one I wanted. She could have had almost any of the lads for miles around but she seemed to favour me. Then the young laird, as Sir Reginald was then, came back home to live at Stavondale. He wanted to enjoy life in those days and he was popular with all the young folks when he came to local dances. Mary was by far the prettiest lassie and she caught his eye. He began to single her out. It turned her head. She really believed he wanted to marry her. Her head was full of dreams of being the next Lady Capel.'

'I can believe that,' William said bitterly. 'Mother was often haughty and she acted as though she was a lady.'

'She only took life easier after you were born, William. We nearly lost her then. Before that she worked tremendously hard. Anyway Sir Victor and Lady Capel had their own ideas about their son's marriage. We never knew whether they forced their son and heir, or whether he was in agreement, but his betrothal was announced to the younger daughter of Lord Drimthorpe. Some of the lassies had been jealous and they were glad to see Mary's rejection,' James reflected sadly. 'Her father was a lot to blame. He had brought her up to believe she was a bit better than the rest of us. She had been away to school in Edinburgh to finish her education and she always dressed in the latest fashions. When she heard about the betrothal she turned her attention back to me. She was determined that we should be married straight away, before Mr Reginald Capel of Stavondale married his bride.'

'Because she was expecting his baby?' William asked, sitting up straight in his seat. This was like hearing stories of strangers he had never met.

'She didna know she was expecting his baby when we married, or at least she wasn't sure, but Maggie was born just over seven months later. Mary said she was premature but she was a fine baby. There were plenty of rumours. Everyone knew how she had set her cap at the young laird. Then we had married hastily. People can be malicious.'

'Surely that's all the more reason why Mother should have shown some understanding, aye, and compassion for Emma.'

'I thought so too,' his father agreed wearily. 'But you have to understand William, she never talked about all this. She never admitted Maggie wasna my daughter. These past weeks when she knew she was dying, her deceit was a burden to her. She said she had cheated me. It was weighing on her conscience . . .'

'And so it should,' William said angrily. 'Do you mean you knew yet you never mentioned it either, Father? Didn't you confront her?'

'There was no point in stirring up trouble. We were married — for better or for worse and I had the woman I wanted. There had never been anyone else for me. Anyway I loved Maggie like my own from the minute she was born. She was the bonniest wee bairn with her mop of coal black hair and big wandering eyes. She lost her baby hair but when it grew again she had a mass of dark curls and rosy cheeks and a wide smile. I remember when she was about ten she stood up in front of the congregation with several other Sunday School children. They all read a lesson from the Bible. I remember thinking how she resembled Sir Reginald's mother, as she used to look when I was a boy. I'm sure he must have thought so too. After the service he spoke to all the children but he took Maggie's hand in his and told her how well she had read.'

'Do you think that's why both Sir Reginald and his son would be at Mother's funeral today?' Jim said. 'Sir Reginald usually leaves everything to do with the estate to his son since Lady Capel died.'

'Maybe. He's getting old, like me,' James Sinclair said.

'All this makes Mother's treatment of Emmie all the more cruel,' William said. 'She wouldn't even have me in the same house when I came back to marry Emma. I would never have come to her funeral if I had known all this.'

'It was not good, the way she acted,' his father agreed. 'Perhaps I should have stuck up for you more, laddie. In truth I didna want ye to leave home, but I've always hated quarrels. Anyway it would have been hell for Emmie if she'd had to live with us, we didn't have a spare cottage then and there was no prospect of any of the farms on this estate coming vacant.'

'I know, Father, I know,' William said, his tone conciliatory. 'I never blamed you, and you were generous with money. I realize that now.'

'I would keep a look out for a farm to rent up here for you, if you wanted to move back?' William saw a pleading look in his father's eyes and lowered his own. There had been many times when he had longed to be able to discuss his problems with his father and Jim, and many times when he yearned for old friends or hearing his mother tongue on market days. He knew he would always be known as 'the Scotchman' and be a bit of an outsider for as long as he lived in Yorkshire, and he also knew how much Emma still missed her family, but he couldn't come back now. They were making their own way, and recently they had managed to put aside a little nest egg for a rainy day. If he returned to Scotland now there would always be some people who thought he had been a failure and come running back for his father's help; there would always be the gossips who would remember he and Emma had not married until after Jamie was born.

'It's too late now, Father. Emmie and I are settled where we are.' He felt, rather than saw, his brother Jim sag with disappointment in the chair beside him.

'Aye, I thought ye'd say that,' his father said with a sigh. 'Now you're here though you might be able to convince Maggie that she should seize her own chance of happiness. She always had a soft spot for you, William. She might listen to you.'

'You mean her happiness with Joe Greig?'

'Yes. Your mother had never told Maggie that I was not her real father until a few days before she died. It's been a big shock to her. I never realized that she expected Maggie to spend all her life working at Bonnybrae to compensate for me giving her a home. I always felt Mary was too possessive but I was aghast when she told me she expected Maggie to repay the debt as she herself had tried to do. It is true she always worked hard and tried to be a good wife and partner for as long as she had her health and strength. In fact I don't know what I would have done without her. It seemed she couldn't die in peace without telling me everything. The trouble is, I believe she has convinced Maggie it is her duty to stay here and look after me and Jim.'

'Surely Maggie must see it's time she lived her own life.'

'I wish she would, but I'm having a job convincing her that she owes me nothing. She's the best daughter a man could have. I had no idea your mother had put such a burden on her.'

Later, when everyone was in bed except him and Jim, William turned to his brother. 'I always wondered why Mother was so possessive with Maggie. She never wanted her to have any male friends, or go to the village dances. She would have been a wonderful mother if she'd had children but it's too late for that now. I hope to God she can find happiness with Joe.'

'It has upset Maggie terribly,' Jim said in troubled tones. 'Joe understood that she would never leave while Mother needed her but I'm almost sure he had hoped they could marry when she died. Maggie has told him about Mother's confession. Joe's initial reaction was that he's not good enough to marry the daughter of the local laird, even though Sir Reginald has never acknowledged her.'

'Of course he's good enough. He's done well at his work and he's a thoroughly kind and decent man. Mind you, we couldn't blame him if he didn't want to marry the laird's bastard.'

'Joe isna like that. None of the Greigs are. You did well when you got Emma for your wife, little brother.'

'I know that. Poor Maggie. She deserves happiness more than anybody I know. Jamie was hoping we would see his Grandfather Greig and Uncle Joe but they didn't come back here for tea after the burial. It's Saturday tomorrow so Joe might be at home. Maybe we could set off early for the train and call to see them? What do you say?'

'That's fine with me. I wish you could stay longer but I know you can't leave Emma with all the work and responsibility. I only hope you can make Maggie see sense.'

'Could you find an excuse not to go to the station, Jim? Maggie would have to drive us then. It would give me time to talk to her and maybe get her and Joe together.'

Maggie was quite willing to drive William and Jamie to the station. She had made them sandwiches for the journey and a box of butterscotch toffee to take back to Meg and the other children. She had kept aside a small packet for Jamie to eat on the train.

'You think of everything, Maggie,' William said. 'Shall I drive there? You will need to drive home again.'

About three quarters of a mile from Bonnybrae the farm track joined the road to Locheagle. On the western boundary of his father's land there was a cluster of derelict buildings in a corner of the field adjoining the road.

'It's strange,' William mused, 'I must have passed that place hundreds of times and never paid attention before. I suppose it would be a small farm at one time but I don't remember anyone ever living there.'

'It was called Braeside. The — the laird added the land, about thirty acres I think, to Bonnybrae when the tenant died. His widow was a Mrs McBurnie. I used to see her working in her garden sometimes when I was a little girl and Jim and I were walking home from school. Even then, the buildings were falling down. She died before you were born and the house has been empty ever since.'

'I'm seeing a lot of things I never noticed before I went away,' William said, flicking the reins to make the pony trot on a little faster. 'I'm glad we shall have a little time to chat with Mr Greig and Joe. Emma will want to hear all their news.'

'I hope everything has gone well while you've been away,' Maggie said. 'I know it's a lot of work for Emmie without you but I'm so glad you came, William.'

'Aye, so am I, Maggie, so am I, if only to see you and Jim and Father. Maybe you and Joe will come down to Yorkshire to see us when you get married.'

'Married? I could never leave Bonnybrae and desert Jim and Father, and Joe is too proud and independent to move in with us.'

'I don't blame him,' William said. 'In fact I think more of him for wanting to be king of his own castle, however humble it might be. Besides, you would be happier living on your own together.'

'Oh William, I couldn't leave F-father when I know how much he's done for Mother, and for me.' A tear trickled silently down her cheek. William glanced behind but Jamie was content to ride in the back of the trap, watching the countryside as they passed. 'I feel lost,' Maggie went on, 'as though I've been cut adrift. I don't know my real father. I mean I know who he is but I don't know him as a person. He is not the anchor in my life as your father has always been — so strong and kind and reliable.'

'Our father. Dry your tears, Maggie. He told me himself he loved you from the moment you were born, even though he knew he had not sired you. He says you're the best daughter a man could have.'

'Then it is even more my duty to stay here and care for him now that he is growing older. Without Mother he needs someone to run his household.' William frowned and chewed his lip.

'Joe loves you, Maggie. He told Emmie he had never expected to find love. He never thought any woman could make him as happy as you do. We both guessed he was waiting to ask you to marry him when you were free from caring for Mother. Do you love him, Maggie?'

'Yes, oh yes, I do,' Maggie said twisting her hands together in agitation, 'but it is impossible now. I must do my duty . . .'

'Of course it isn't impossible. Neither Father nor Jim expect you to sacrifice your happiness for them. Mother has deprived you enough already. They both believe you deserve to be happily married. They like Joe. He is a good man.' William fell silent as they drew into Locheagle village. He was frustrated. He had not made much of a job of persuading Maggie that she should grasp her happiness in both hands and marry Joe. He wondered if Joe expected Maggie to move in with him and live at the cottage in Locheagle. He wouldn't be being unreasonable. Mr Greig was the same age as his own father and a widower too. At least their father would have Jim for company whereas Emmie's father would be alone if Joe moved out. What a tangle life was when people had responsibilities.

Julie was already at the cottage with her three children. She greeted them warmly and in no time at all his cousins were whisking Jamie off to the garden to see if the lettuce and radishes had grown which they had helped Granddad Greig to sow.

'He made a wee house with glass specially to keep them warm,' five-year-old Dora said.

'Joe told me you usually bring them some freshly baked bread and scones on a Saturday morning, Julie,' Maggie said. 'I know how much they appreciate your help.'

'It's a pleasure and in return, Davy's father keeps us supplied with fresh vegetables most of the year.'

'Ye'll have time for a cup of tea before ye leave for the station, William?' Mr Greig offered. 'I'll go and see the wee rascals are not digging up the soil to see how the plants are growing first. We only planted them under the cloches last Saturday.'

'Will you show me the potatoes you planted, Joe?' William asked, seizing the opportunity to talk to his brother-in-law alone. Joe nodded and led the way to the far end of the garden, nearest the road.

'I've never seen Maggie look so ill and tired,' William said without wasting time on small talk. 'She admits she loves you, Joe. I hope to God you can talk some sense into her and persuade her to marry you.'

'I think you know there's nothing I want more,' Joe said, 'but Maggie has such a strong sense of duty and now she knows your father has brought her up without ever hinting she's the daughter of another man, she is convinced she owes him a huge debt. She says she must stay at Bonnybrae and look after him and Jim. Even before Mrs Sinclair died, your father told me I would be welcome to live at Bonnybrae too. I expect you think I'm stubborn and ungrateful but I want Maggie to myself in our own home, by our own fireside.'

‘I don’t think you’re stubborn or ungrateful, Joe. Have you asked Maggie to come to live at Locheagle with you and your father?’

‘No. I know Maggie wouldn’t want to be so far away, especially now. Anyway Father made it plain when we travelled back on the train together, that he would be content to live alone so long as we all call to see him regularly. And of course we would. Ye’ve seen how good Julie is, and Maggie was just as kind and generous before her mother became such a heavy burden.’

‘I know I shouldna speak ill of the dead, and especially not about my own mother,’ William said, kicking viciously at a loose stone, ‘but she was a selfish, demanding woman and she was completely unreasonable with me and Emmie, especially considering her own past. She has made Maggie feel she was a burden to my father and she must repay him. He doesn’t want that at all. He told me he understands how you feel about having your own fireside. He would help you get a cottage to rent if that’s what you would like and if you can persuade Maggie.’

‘I have enough money to build a cottage if we could find a bit of land convenient to Bonnybrae, and for me to get to my work every day,’ Joe said. ‘I’ve been able to save a bit of money since I’ve been manager at Courton’s and I don’t want to let Mr Courton down, even if I was ready to give up earning my living. I have not told anyone yet, not even Maggie. Truth is we have had no opportunity to discuss anything recently. Mr Courton wants to make me a partner with him on condition that I will stay with him until he’s ready to retire. That will not be for a good few years yet. He doesn’t want to be taken over by one of the big weaving firms. That would suit me all right but persuading Maggie to marry me is my big problem,’ Joe said unhappily. ‘Perhaps a man can’t have everything in life.’

‘Everybody deserves some happiness,’ William said firmly, ‘and nobody deserves it more than Maggie and you, Joe. Two decent people trying their best to live a good life and earn a decent living. I don't know what Emmie will say when I tell her about the skeletons in my family cupboard, or the consequences. I know she longs to see you and Maggie married. She would love to see you both if you could come to visit us together.'

'I can't see an easy solution at present,' Joe said dejectedly, 'but it doesn't mean I shall give up trying.'

'Are you two coming for a drink of tea?' Julie called from the doorway.

'Maggie says it will soon be time to leave if you intend to catch the train.' Jamie was reluctant to leave his grandfather and cousins.

'I'm coming too, laddie,' Bert Greig assured him with a smile. 'You run ahead and get your hands washed. Your Aunt Julie has brought a lovely cake and I spy your Uncle Davy coming down the road to get a piece too. You'd better hurry.'

Once they were seated round the kitchen table with Maggie and Julie pouring tea and passing around scones and cakes Bert Greig said, 'This lad o' yours would be a fine help to me and my garden, William, if only you lived nearer.'

'Grandfather Sinclair said he wished we lived nearer as well,' Jamie said, swallowing the last crumb of cake. 'He said I would make a grand shepherd for him if I learn to train the collie dogs as well as you did, Father.' His tone was wistful and William guessed he was not yet ready to go back to Yorkshire. Although they had come for a sad occasion, everyone had spoken kindly to Jamie and made him welcome. It made a change for him to see so many relations.

William longed to be back home with Emmie, to feel her arms around his neck and her lips soft and yielding to his kisses. He felt a bit depressed as the train carried them south. The way things were, Maggie and Joe would never find such happiness together and he had done nothing to help them. He found having to sit for five hours or more very tedious. He wanted to make the train go faster. He had a lot to tell Emmie. She would be as shocked and angered as he was by his mother's deceit and her use of Maggie to salve her own conscience. She had showed no compassion or understanding to Emmie yet her own situation would have been worse if his father had not married her. Why had she grown so bitter in recent years?

'Father! You were miles away,' Jamie interrupted his thoughts. 'I asked you how much longer it will be before we get home. Can I eat some of my butterscotch toffee now?'

'I'm sorry, my thoughts were back in Scotland. Yes, you can eat your toffee. Can you spare a piece for me? I remember your Aunt Maggie making toffee for me when I was about your age.' Jamie held out the packet while his father selected a small piece.

'I hope we can go back to visit again soon,' Jamie said. 'It would be great if Uncle Joe and Aunt Maggie get married to each other. They would both make us welcome then.'

'I pray they will find a solution so they can be together too,' William said with feeling, 'but I wish I could have done something to help solve their problems.'

'What sort of problems? Can't they do what they want when they're both grown up? I shall marry whoever I want when I'm a man.' William gave a faint smile.

'Problems don't disappear just because people are adults, laddie. Sometimes they have more problems.'

'What sort of problems do Uncle Joe and Aunt Maggie have?'

'Your Aunt Maggie has too much conscience; she is a kind hearted person and she is grateful to your grandfather for looking after her so well all these years.'

'But that's what fathers and mothers do when they get children.'

'Cliff Barnes' mother didn't look after him. She let his stepfather beat him cruelly. That's why he can't use his brain as well as most people. He was so unhappy and frightened that he ran away. Polly and Tom's mother died when they were quite young so she couldn't look after them. There's nothing certain in life. Anyway Maggie thinks she should continue living at Bonnybrae to look after Grandfather

Sinclair now he's getting old and doesn't have a wife to look after him anymore, but Uncle Joe wants her to live with him in a house of their own. The trouble is he needs to catch the train every morning to go to his work so he couldn't live any further away from a station than he does now. As it is, he walks three miles to the station every morning and three miles back to Locheagle at night.'

'Oh, I see.' Jamie was silent for a while, staring out of the window as they chugged through the Dales. He liked seeing the sheep grazing peacefully on the slopes. They passed a cluster of cottages right beside the railway line. 'Mr Thorpe, at school, says there will soon be railways everywhere because they're growing like a giant spider's web over the country.'

'I expect he's right. There are a lot more now than when I was your age.'

'I heard you asking Aunt Maggie about that broken-down house we passed on the way to Grandfather Greig's. Maybe the owner could repair it and then Uncle Joe could rent it for him and Aunt Maggie to live in? She could go to the farm every day then if she wanted. Maybe Uncle Joe could get a ride to the station with Uncle Jim when he takes the milk to the train?' William stared at his son for a moment, his mouth falling open in surprise.

'My goodness, Jamie, you have been keeping your ears and eyes open, just as Garridan keeps telling me you do. He says you don't miss a thing. You've certainly had the best idea so far. At least we could suggest it. The ruins are on the Stavondale estate so your Grandfather Sinclair would need to ask the laird if he would repair the cottage. What did Maggie call it?'

'Braeside, I think. If it belongs to the laird he must have plenty of money to make it into a house again. Do you think Uncle Joe could afford to pay the rent?'

'I'm sure he could.' William said. 'As soon as we get home we'll tell your mother all about it and ask her if she will write a letter to Maggie and one to Joe and tell them both what a bright idea you've had. I will write to Grandfather

Sinclair and tell him too. I'm sure he will ask Mr Capel the Younger if he will rebuild the house.'

'Is Mr Capel the laird?'

'Not exactly, but he manages the estate I believe. He's Sir Reginald Capel's son. When his father dies the estate will belong to him. He will be Sir Roger Capel of Stavondale then.'

Emma was relieved to see William and Jamie safely home again, but everything had gone smoothly in their absence and she was flushed with success at managing so well. William looked at her rosy cheeks and bright eyes and all he wanted to do was carry her up to the privacy of their bedroom and love her as she deserved, but of course he had to wait in an agony of impatience until bedtime. Neither could he explain the state of Maggie's mind and her conviction that it was her duty to spend the rest of her life caring for his father.

He had expected Emma to be as angry and indignant about his mother as he was himself. She found it difficult to believe that the stern, proud woman who had been so devout had had the same weaknesses, committed the same sins, as herself and William.

'I suppose there would have been rumours if we had stayed there,' she said simply. 'All I want is to let the past be forgotten and I pray to God it never makes either of us as bitter and unforgiving. The one thing I can't forgive is that she has made Maggie pay for her own debt to your father, if he even considered she owed him a debt. It is worse if she is supposed to go on paying for the rest of her life.'

William was convinced Jamie had found a solution for Joe and Maggie so he was bitterly disappointed when Emma received Maggie's reply.

Thank you for thinking about Joe and me and our happiness, and please tell Jamie it was a brilliant idea. A cottage at Braeside would have been an ideal solution. Father thinks so too. He has made an appointment to see Mr Roger Capel tomorrow but he doesn't hold much hope of him agreeing. Apparently Father asked if the estate would repair the cottage when Mrs McBurnie died. He wanted to use it for a married worker at Bonnybrae because both Annie and Robin wanted to marry within the year and would be leaving Bonnybrae. The young laird was beginning to take over managing the estate then. He said Sir Reginald had been too indulgent with his tenants in the past and he had already added the extra land to Bonnybrae. He flatly refused to waste money on a derelict building when we have a perfectly good bothy for single men. Father says he was very disappointed at the time but we managed without his cooperation. All the land and cottages from the outskirts of Locheagle village to beyond East Lowrie belong to the Stavondale estate, even if there had been anything suitable.

Maggie wrote a few more sentences but Emma felt her letter was shorter and more stilted than usual; almost dejected. Her heart ached for both her and Joe.

CHAPTER EIGHT

It was as James Sinclair had expected. Mr Roger Capel barely took time to listen to his request. He refused to consider any changes involving the ruins of what had once been Braeside Farm.

'It is true the pigsties and the small barn are derelict now, but surely the cottage could be made habitable if it had a new roof and repairs to the doors and windows,' James reasoned quietly. 'You would be getting a rent in return. Joe Greig is a decent honest man with a steady job.'

'Then let him rent a cottage somewhere else.' Mr Capel raised his voice more than he realized and pushed back his chair with such force it fell to the floor. The truth was he and his wife liked lavish entertainment and Roger couldn't wait for his father to die so he could have the estate completely in his hands. He planned to sell some of the outlying farms to raise capital and settle their debts. Meanwhile there were constant arguments, so he had no intention of spending money on derelict buildings.

James left the estate office closing the door quietly behind him. He wondered if the rumours were true that there was strife between the young laird and his wife. He had dismissed the talk as servants' gossip when he had heard it at the cattle market, but Mr Roger Capel was certainly in bad humour. He swallowed hard. Although he had been prepared for a refusal he was as disappointed as he knew Joe and Maggie would be. He would have to persuade Maggie he didn't need her to keep house for him and Jim, but how would he do that without making her feel unwanted? Perhaps he could put one of those notices in the paper asking for a suitable woman but he shuddered at the prospect of having a stranger living in his home, organizing his food and washing and cleaning, making his bed, ironing his shirts.

'Good morning, James. You're looking very downcast. I was sorry to hear of your wife's — of Mary's death.'

'Thank you, Sir Reginald. She had not been in good health for some time.'

'No, we have not seen her with you in the kirk in recent years although she used to be the most regular attender. Nothing else going wrong at Bonnybrae I hope?' He had heard his son's voice raised in anger. He was curious but he knew Roger would call him an interfering old man, or worse, if he questioned him.

'No, nothing wrong. I was here to ask if there was any possibility of the estate repairing the roof and windows on the old house at Braeside and renting it to Joe Greig. He and Maggie would like to get married. Unfortunately Mary convinced Maggie it is her duty to stay at Bonnybrae and look after Jim and me. I've tried to tell her that's nonsense and she must grasp her chance of happiness with Joe. He has a good job as manager at Courton's so he needs to live where he can get the train each day. Braeside would have been a fine compromise and suited them both.'

'Aah, I'm pleased to hear Maggie would like to marry now her mother has gone. I'm sure she will make a fine wife.'

'Yes, she deserves some happiness. She has been a good daughter. Joe is the son of Bert Greig. You may remember Bert?'

'Bert Greig . . .' He wrinkled his brow in thought. 'Yes, I think I do. He married a pretty little girl called Lizzie. They only had eyes for each other when we were young. Is that the one?'

'It is. They have brought up four children to be thrifty and hard working. Joe tells me he could afford to renovate the house himself but I told him he would be spending his own money to make it habitable and then have to pay rent for it because it belongs to the Stavondale estate. Anyway it seems he wouldna get permission to do anything with it,' James concluded, unaware how disappointed he sounded.

'Is that what you were seeing my son about? I told him last spring that Braeside is an eyesore and he should either repair it or have the stone carted away so the land can be returned to pasture. Surely he is pleased to know he will have a good tenant as soon as the repairs are done?'

'No. He says he would not waste money on such a project,' James said, his mouth tightening. The young laird had barely waited to hear what he had to say.

'He is refusing to repair it?' Sir Reginald scowled. He leaned more heavily on his stick. 'You say this man, Joe Greig, will be a good husband for Maggie?' He looked James straight in the eye. He had never acknowledged that Maggie was his daughter and James knew he never would, but they both knew the truth.

'He is a good, decent man. He and Maggie are very happy when they're together. He is clever with his hands too. He has repaired several of the doors and windows in the buildings at Bonnybrae and he refuses to take any payment. He said it gave him satisfaction to see them neat and tidy again. He would have been a good tenant.'

'I'm sure you're right, James. You always were a good judge of men and horses. I trust your opinion.' Sir Reginald drew himself up taller as though reaching a decision. 'I know you're one of the best tenants we have so I shall ask my lawyer to visit me as soon as he can. If it can be done I shall ask him to draw up a deed for the land on which the Braeside house and outbuildings stand and I shall put it into the name of Maggie Sinclair. I would like you to keep this matter strictly between ourselves until the deed is done. Also there is one condition . . .'

'And that is?' James Sinclair asked warily, yet barely able to contain his amazement and excitement.

'The house must be repaired and the whole site tidied up again as soon as possible at the expense of the man Maggie intends to marry but in return it will be their own property, in their name. I shall include a clause stating that if ever it is sold, the Stavondale estate will have the first chance to buy it at a fair market price.'

'I know Joe and Maggie will make the whole place look cared for. That sounds very fair, and very generous to me,' James Sinclair said jubilantly. 'This news will make both Maggie and Joe very happy indeed.'

Sir Reginald held his gaze steadily in silence for a moment or two, then almost under his breath he said, 'We both know it is the very least I can do for her.' Then more briskly, 'You may tell them, but you must ask them to wait until they hear from my lawyer and the papers are signed before they begin any work. Keep it to yourselves until then. I am afraid my son will not be happy about this, but he's not the laird yet. Only God knows what he will do with his inheritance when I am gone or if there will be anything left for his own son and daughter.' He sighed heavily, then turned and grasping his cane he walked stiffly away, leaving James to collect his horse from the hitching post.

He could scarcely wait to get back to Bonnybrae and tell Maggie what had transpired, although he took care to warn her she and Joe must keep the business a secret until Sir Reginald had signed the deeds passing it to them. Later he confided in Jim, telling him of Mr Capel the Younger of Stavondale's angry refusal.

'There are rumours that he and his wife owe money to most of the local tradesmen,' Jim said. 'He's not very amenable as a landlord already when it comes to repairs, so I don't know how we shall manage when he does inherit the estate. He will not be happy with us when he discovers the arrangement his father has made over Braeside.'

'Ye're right there, Jim,' his father said slowly. 'When he inherits I reckon the first thing he will do will be to increase our rents.'

'Aye, I suppose so. He can't cut back on repairs because the estate has not done any since he started overseeing things instead of the factor. Bonnybrae is not the only farm he has neglected. The strange thing is, he does spend money improving the four small farms bordering East Lowrie village.'

'He's a different generation. I suppose he has different ideas and priorities to his father and grandfather.'

Sir Reginald Capel lost no time in sending a letter to his lawyer asking him to call at Stavondale Tower at his earliest convenience. His father and grandfather had dealt with the same firm of lawyers. Charles MacQuade was two years younger than himself and they had known each other since their Edinburgh schooldays. MacQuade had a family of four daughters before he got a son, Neil. Fortunately the young MacQuade was following in the footsteps of his father and grandfather and Sir Reginald was pleased to meet him when they accepted his invitation to lunch at Stavondale Tower. Not for the first time, Sir Reginald was pleased Roger and his wife had insisted on setting up house on their own in the west wing, even though it had cost a fortune making it suit their taste in comfort and elegance.

Charles MacQuade made no comment but he raised his bushy eyebrows in surprise when he heard Sir Reginald Capel was disposing of even such a small part of the Stavondale estate. Sir Reginald had no reason to justify his actions to anyone but for some reason he found himself explaining that he felt he owed a debt to Maggie Sinclair, although he had never acknowledged her as his daughter to anyone before, even to the man who had brought her up and treated her in every respect as his own child. Charles MacQuade simply nodded. In his business he encountered many such situations.

'I would not have considered granting her the deed to the site,' he went on, 'but Sinclair asked my son if he would renovate the property and rent it to the girl and her husband.

Roger refused to consider such a thing. He didn't even consult me, but then he never does these days. He can't wait for me to join my wife in the kirk yard.' He didn't notice MacQuade and his son exchange glances.

He continued, 'According to James Sinclair, Joe Greig has enough money of his own, and the ability to oversee the rebuilding of the house himself, with the help of a builder from Locheagle, but as Sinclair advised, there would be no point in using his own money to restore the dwelling house, then have to pay a rent for doing so. So, you see now why I want a deed drawn up nice and tightly in the name of Maggie Sinclair, making sure Braeside and the plot of land on which it stands, including the garden and the derelict buildings, legally belong to her and her husband.'

'Did you say the man's name was Joseph Greig from Locheagle?'

'Yes I did. Is there something I should know about him?'

'Only that Mr Courton has made him a partner in the mill and the Courton business. We drew up the agreement, didn't we Neil?'

'Yes Father, I drew it up myself. Mr Courton has a high opinion of Mr Joseph Greig. He wants to make sure he will stay with him, as his partner, until Courton, or both of them, are ready to give up and sell out to one of the big textile firms.'

'Courton does seem to have a great word of the young man,' Charles MacQuade reflected. 'He has grown to rely on him with so many new developments in machinery and modernisation. Apparently Greig started at the bottom when he left school. He has worked himself up and he gets on well with the workers. So far they have had no trouble with workers' protests.'

'I see. I am pleased to hear that. It convinces me I am right to help the couple find a home and security.'

When they had discussed the finer points and Neil had made adequate notes and agreed to have the site measured officially, Charles MacQuade cleared his throat.

'I was pleased to get your summons, Reginald. I thought perhaps you had taken your business over the road to our competitors.'

'To Roseman and Gordon? Why in heaven's name would I do that? Our families have worked well together for two — or is it three? — generations now. I am glad to see your son is following in the family tradition. I have not had any legal matters to discuss since my wife died.'

'I understand that . . .' Charles hesitated then went on. 'Presumably you haven't heard that your son has taken his legal business to Roseman and Gordon?'

'What? What legal matters could he have to discuss? Except perhaps drawing up his will I suppose now he has a son and a daughter. But why would he go there?'

'It was not his will he wanted to discuss. He approached Neil first. Fortunately my son felt his proposition was bordering on dishonesty so he came to me for advice before suggesting Roger should not proceed down the route he was proposing. I gather he lost his temper, Neil?'

'Yes, he did,' Neil agreed, in response to his father's questioning eyebrows. 'Some of his creditors were impatient for their money. One of them was threatening to take him to court. He wanted us to sell two of the outlying farms on the Stavondale estate. To do so he proposed to forge your signature or have us make a case for you being of unsound mind.'

'I am very pleased to see there is absolutely nothing wrong with your mind, Reginald,' Charles MacQuade said, striving for a lighter note.

'But this is preposterous!' Sir Reginald almost exploded. 'How has the situation been resolved?'

'We don't know. He went to Roseman. I doubt if either he or his partner would agree to do what he wanted but they may have arranged a loan on the strength of his future inheritance. Enough to keep his creditors quiet apparently. Certainly none of the farms have been sold. We hold the deeds, as you know.'

'Thank God for that,' Sir Reginald said. 'I knew Roger and his wife were spending more than his allowance, which is more than generous I might tell you. He asked for more and I gave it to them at first. Twice recently I have refused his requests.' He rubbed his temple. 'If he is already borrowing money on the strength of his expectations there is no doubt he will sell some of the farms as soon as I'm gone. There will be nothing left for my grandchildren. My grandson is a fine wee fellow. He reminds me of my father. He's named after him too, Jonathan Robert. His sister Catherine is three years younger, a pretty wee thing, but a bit of a daredevil for a girl. I fear she has inherited my own stubborn character. They are both at school in Edinburgh. Is there anything I can do to protect Stavondale and ensure they get some sort of an inheritance?'

'If you're serious about this, Reginald, then Neil and I will give the matter some consideration. When we have drawn up the deeds for Braeside I will bring them for your signature, along with one of my clerks to act as an independent witness. That would be better than using Neil, or one of your staff in case there is trouble in the future when you, or I — maybe both of us — are no longer here. In law it is better to leave nothing to chance. I'm glad we have had this meeting today. We both know now what we're dealing with and hopefully we shall be prepared.'

'A family trust might be the answer,' Neil suggested, 'with trustees who would protect the interests of your grandchildren.'

'We must discuss it as soon as possible,' Sir Reginald said, rising stiffly to his feet. 'As you see I'm an old man these days so get back to me as soon as you can. I may not have as much time left as I would like. I don't want to take any chances.'

CHAPTER NINE

Sir Reginald wrote a personal letter to James Sinclair, confirming his intentions regarding Braeside but asking him to keep the information within his close family until the deed was signed.

James confided in Maggie and Joe, and also in Jim. Maggie was jubilant. If they could live at Braeside it was the very best compromise for her to care for the three men she loved.

'Hey, Maggie, I'd hate you to be disappointed,' Jim warned with brotherly affection. 'Don't make any plans until you have the deed in writing.'

'Sir Reginald Capel is a man of his word, and a gentleman,' James Sinclair said. 'He will keep his promise.'

'I'm sure he intends to keep it, Father,' Jim said, 'but you have to admit he is getting an old man.'

'He is only a few years older than I am,' his father said indignantly.

'Maybe he is but he hasna led a healthy life like you. Anyway I can guess the young laird will try to put a stop to it and these legal things seem to take forever.'

'Mr Capel had his chance to deal with Braeside himself,' his father said. 'He refused to listen to any suggestions.'

'I know. I reckon he has problems of his own to sort before he will consider the likes of us.'

'What sort of problems can he have that would prevent him allowing Maggie and Joe to make a decent home from a derelict house?'

'I've heard rumours that he and his wife owe money all over the place,' Jim said. 'I don't know whether they're true but I do know neither Mr Fletcher, the butcher, nor Monteith, the grocer at East Lowrie, will deliver supplies to them.'

Maggie knew Jim's caution was well founded but she couldn't suppress her excitement and wrote Emma and William a more cheerful letter than she had managed for weeks.

Give Jamie several big hugs from me. Tell him he made a brilliant suggestion when he thought of Braeside. Joe says we shall always have a room for him if he wants to visit. He plans to build us a bathroom with a flush toilet and hot and cold water for bathing. Won't that be wonderful instead of filling and emptying the tin bath? Tell Jamie he will have to be our first visitor.

Maggie had no idea that Jamie would read, and remember, her words.

The MacQuades proceeded with all speed to draw up the deed for the Braeside house plus a generous area for a garden front and back, as well as the old piggeries, space for a hen run and a tool shed. It was young Mr MacQuade who came in person to measure out the area and he insisted on helping Joe hammer in far more marker pegs than Joe himself would have considered necessary.

'I would advise you to put up a good strong fence all round before you do anything else, Mr Greig,' Neil MacQuade said, 'and if you should encounter any trouble from anyone please let us know. We are doing this on the orders of Sir Reginald Capel of Stavondale himself.'

Mr Roger Capel rode up to Braeside in a blind fury the day after the postman delivered a sealed and signed copy of the deeds, with written permission to start rebuilding. He tried to get his horse to kick out the marker pegs and when that failed, he jumped off and started kicking at them himself, but there were a lot of them and they were firmly hammered in as Neil MacQuade had instructed. It was a Saturday and Maggie was very glad Joe was there. He remained calm and reasonable in the face of Mr Capel's anger and foul language.

'We have the full authority of Sir Reginald Capel,' Joe said quietly. 'If you have any objections to our taking over the site and rebuilding the house then you must discuss the matter with him.'

'He is a senile old man! He doesn't know what he's doing. Remove these pegs at once and I shall deal with the matter myself.' Joe understood then why Mr MacQuade had suggested he should fence the perimeter of the agreed area and he made that his first task. They did not see Mr Capel again but rumours of his anger and displeasure with his father circulated amongst his workers and quickly spread into the wider world, inevitably gaining additions as they were repeated. James Sinclair was thankful the old laird had kept his word for Maggie's sake. He must have guessed his son would try to overturn his plans when he had made sure everything was done legally. He couldn't help a small smile as he wondered what the young laird would say if he ever learned Maggie was his half-sister.

Every week Maggie's letters to Emma and William were full of news about developments at the house, although she never forgot to send news of Emma's father and the rest of the family. Emma was glad of this as she missed her mother's letters. Julie was also a good correspondent but Emma knew there would always be an empty space in her heart for her mother.

Joe had listened to the advice of Mrs Courton, the wife of his employer, now his partner. She and her husband had travelled to various parts of the country and twice to France. She invited Joe and Maggie to lunch one Sunday and suggested they build the house as big as they could afford but they must be sure to install a hot water system and have a bathroom with a flush toilet.

It was Emma's father who made a big effort to write and tell her that Joe's new house had three bedrooms upstairs as well as one of the new-fangled bathtubs with hot water from the tap and a drain to take it away. It also had two downstairs rooms as well as a large kitchen, a pantry, and a wash house with a flush toilet.

'Maggie is a kindly young woman,' he wrote. 'She insists they have plenty of room for me to live with them if I feel the least bit lonely or if I am ill. 'Tis comforting to know but they deserve some time on their own and I'm happy in my ain wee cottage.'

As soon as the house was finished and furnished to his satisfaction Joe refused to wait a moment longer to make Maggie his wife. It was Maggie's heart's desire too, but she made time to write to Emma.

Dearest Emmie,

I do believe Joe would get me the moon if that were possible. He has thought of everything to make my life as happy and pleasant as it can be. I wish with all my heart that you and William and the children could be with us for our wedding but I know that is impossible, especially when you are expecting another baby in May. We both know you already have so much work to do inside and out. It will be a very quiet wedding with Davy as Joe's best man and my sister Bessie as matron of honour. Julie's father has agreed to marry us in Locheagle church at ten o'clock on the morning of Friday the eleventh of March, 1910.

Dear Julie insists she will provide some light refreshments before we catch the train for Ayr where we shall spend one night before we return home together to Braeside. I never thought I could feel so happy.

Father employed a second horseman in November and he lives in the cottage next to Mr and Mrs Edgar. They have three children. His wife is called Edna and she is thirty-six. She is going to help me in the house at Bonnybrae. Father insists I must give my attention to Joe now but he will be at work during the day so I'm sure I shall be able to look after all of my menfolk and keep them happy and content. I do hope so anyway.

Maggie added a few more lines and her excitement and happiness seemed to spring from the page.

'I feel almost homesick,' Emma told William with a sigh, 'but I'm glad they understand we could not possibly attend the wedding. You must help me find a lovely gift for them.'

'That may not be so easy when they are so far away. We don't want anything which might break. We will go to Wakefield together and choose something. It seems strange your brother marrying my sister, Emmie. It binds our families closer than ever.' He grinned wickedly. 'I wonder what my mother would have said.'

Emma smiled and made no reply. They both knew how strongly Mary Sinclair would have disapproved.

Emma's baby was born earlier than expected. On 6 May news spread around the country of the death of King Edward VII from pneumonia. Usually Emma showed a keen interest in anything to do with the royal family and it was only nine years since the death of his mother, Queen Victoria.

'He seems to have been king for such a short time,' she murmured absently. William raised his eyebrows at her apparent lack of interest but Emma felt too uneasy and restless to notice. All day her back ached and from time to time pains racked her stomach, then disappeared. She thought it was too early for the baby to be born but she knew something was not right. She had never needed a doctor at any of the births. The local midwife had always managed with Polly's assistance, providing hot water and towels and whatever was needed. All night she was uneasy, unaware that William heard her faint moans of distress and felt alarmed. Emmie had never been a woman who made a fuss. When dawn broke, he spoke softly.

'Shall I send for the doctor, Emmie? Do you think it's the baby?'

‘I don’t know. I’m sure it should not be born yet.’

‘I’ll send Jamie for the doctor . . .’

‘No! No, don’t do that. I don’t want a doctor. Just let me rest. Can you manage the milking without me?’

‘Of course we can, dearest Emmie, if you’re sure you will be all right. I know Polly doesn’t like milking but she’ll lend a hand this morning and Meg is almost as good as you or me. I wish Jamie would show more interest in the cows instead of hankering after a flock of ewes and lambs.’ He bit back any further complaints about his eldest son as he saw beads of sweat coat Emmie’s brow and watched her bite hard on her lower lip to stifle the moan of pain.

Things were still the same by mid-afternoon and the midwife asked William to send for the doctor.

‘This is the eighth baby your wife has borne and I’ve been with her for them all, except your first lad. She is one of the best mothers I know and she never makes a fuss. Something is not right, lad. The baby isn’t big but it isn’t coming right.’

William lost no time in harnessing the pony and trap so that he could bring the doctor back with him. His face was pale. He didn’t know what he would do if he lost Emmie, and women did die in childbirth, he knew that. He had never seen Emmie like this before.

CHAPTER TEN

The baby was in a breach position but Doctor Dunhill soon realized even that was not straightforward.

'We shall need to use forceps,' he muttered in a low voice to the midwife.

'Oh dear,' Ida Thorpe fretted. 'I've never had trouble with Mrs Sinclair before, Doctor. She's one of the best mothers I attend.'

'That may be so but this one is not so straightforward as we would like. I'm going to give her chloroform.'

'No!' Emma protested but her voice was weak and she wondered if they had heard her. 'No,' she said again.

'It's for the best,' Doctor Dunhill said kindly. 'After all, they gave it to the old Queen and I'm sure you need it now as much as she did.' Emma had neither the strength nor time to protest further. When she regained consciousness, she heard the doctor speaking as though from a great distance.

'The baby was a boy, Mr Sinclair, but he lived barely ten minutes. I am sorry.'

'Never mind the baby,' William said with unusual sharpness. 'How is my wife? Is she — is she going to be all right?' he asked, his voice ending in a husky croak. Emma tried to tell him she was fine, but no sound came.

'Your wife will need a lot of rest and nourishing food, Mr Sinclair. Mrs Thorpe tells me she usually copes exceedingly well with the birth of her babies but this was no ordinary birth and she has lost a lot of blood. It will take some months before she regains her usual strength and good health. I strongly advise you to make sure she does not start having any more babies for at least a year, if you value her life.'

'Oh I do, indeed I don't know how any of us would manage without her,' William said, speaking more openly than was his habit. The doctor nodded.

'You will probably find your wife will be down in spirits after her ordeal and with no living baby at the end of it to suckle and bring her comfort. Do your best to cheer her. I understand from Mr Rowbottom, the agent for Lord Hanley, that you are a very busy man, but . . .'

'I shall do whatever I can to get Emmie well again, and happy,' William said fervently. 'Thank you both for saving her life.'

Emma couldn't understand the dreadful tiredness that seemed to affect her for months after the birth. The doctor was right about her swings in mood. William confided his anxiety over Emma to Drew Kerr one day when they met at the cattle market, but he and Annie had no experience of losing a baby and Drew could offer little advice.

The time to gather the hay had come round again and Garridan and his relative, Fred, came to help gather in the crop, as had become their habit each year, in return for a small stack built on the common for their own use. This year their uncle had died while they were in Ireland and William really missed the old man's help with sharpening the pointed knives for the mowing machine. Each evening he worked late sharpening the knives himself to get a good start for the following day but it troubled him that he was leaving Emma so much alone once the children were in bed, although she still had Polly for company with their knitting and mending that never seemed to be finished. One evening he suggested she should come outside and talk to him while he worked. He made her a wooden seat, padded with a sack of sweet smelling hay. They began to enjoy this quiet time alone together and a new, deeper companionship developed, binding them even more closely than their earlier passion as their conversation ranged over many topics.

William met his half-cousin, Drew Kerr, at the market from time to time if they happened to be selling or buying animals on the same day. Both men enjoyed the challenge of doing a good deal, but both had reason to be proud of the stock they bred and reared. They had one such meeting on a cold day in December and decided to go for a pie and a drink of ale together, since both had got a good trade.

'It's a good thing we shall soon be seeing the end of this year,' Drew said. 'There's been nothing but turmoil, what with the King's death and now all the upset in Parliament. God knows what two elections in the year must have cost the country.'

'Aye, and I believe they have ended up the same again with two hundred and seventy-two seats to the Liberals and the same to the Tories. All the trouble was over the Budget and the House of Lords and it doesn't look as though there can be much change. Emma is all in favour of the Suffragettes and women having a vote.' William grinned ruefully. 'She gets quite steamed up about it but she is sure women would have more idea about running things.'

'She could be right at that,' Drew agreed. 'I wonder what King George thinks to it all. It can't be easy for him with so much unrest in the country.'

'No, it was a bit worrying with the dockers going on strike and the miners supporting them.'

'Don't forget the cotton workers too. Seven hundred cotton mills were closed. All that must have made a difference to trade. Anyway, we'd better forget the rest of the world and think about our own families. Annie always gets nostalgic and a bit homesick around New Year. She misses our old customs. She gave me a letter for Emma. She hopes you will all come to visit us on Boxing Day for dinner at noon.' He handed William a letter.

It had taken both families some time to adjust to celebrating Christmas instead of New Year, as they had been accustomed to do back home in Scotland.

'I am glad Annie didn't ask us for Christmas Day,' Emma said. 'Polly might have gone to the Wrights but she and Maisie Blackford and Cliff are like part of our family now. They depend on us for the Christmas festivity.'

'I'm not sure how many of us will be able to go to Blakemore anyway,' William said. 'The poor old pony couldn't take us all, even if we could squeeze into the trap. Jamie is growing into a big laddie these days and even Meg is almost as tall as you, Emmie.'

'Well, I never was very tall,' Emma said ruefully. 'If Jamie and Meg rode together on one of the Clydesdales, could the rest of us get in the trap? Or perhaps we should leave Janet at home. She is not two years old yet and she doesn't understand about sitting still for such a long journey. I'm sure Polly would be happy to keep her and we shall have to be home in time for the milking, and their bedtime.'

'Aye, ye're right. It will be a long ride there and back, and a short visit at this time of year,' William agreed. 'I think Annie looks forward to the company though. Drew says she still gets homesick for Scotland, even after all these years. Maybe we should leave young Peter at home as well. He'll be company for Janet.'

'Yes, I suppose so,' Emma agreed. 'He will be three at the end of December so I could tell him we shall bring him a birthday present.'

As it happened, Annie's favourite housecat had three fluffy white kittens so she was happy to send one of them to a good home. Peter claimed it as his pet and named it Snowball.

The Kerrs' eldest son, Ranald, was seventeen, four years older than Jamie. As soon as they had finished eating their meal on Boxing Day, he said he had arranged to meet one of his friends to see if they could catch a glimpse of the hunt, and maybe even the fox if they came towards Wilmore village.

'They often come this way because our landlord is all in favour of them hunting over his farms, so long as they don't upset the ewes at lambing time. Do you want to come, Jamie? Bill has a young cousin staying with him, a bit of a mardy, sullen fellow he says but he has to entertain him. I think he's about your age and he comes from somewhere near Joe Wright's, your blacksmith.'

Jamie was eager to accompany his older cousin. He was used to walking three miles to school and back, as well as roaming over the common with Garridan and the other gypsies when they were catching rabbits, or when he was trying to train Jill, his very own collie. Exercise was no trouble to him.

'Well don't stay away too long or you'll find yourself walking home,' William warned sternly. 'Remember we have to be back for the milking and it is dark early.'

'Yes, Dad,' Jamie muttered and pulled a face at Ranald. 'Cows are all my father thinks about,' he said when they were out of earshot.

'Don't you like cows then?' Ranald asked.

'I don't mind any of the animals but I hate sitting there for ages milking,' Jamie admitted. 'I wish we could have had a flock of breeding sheep. Grandfather Sinclair has sheep up in Scotland. He said I could go and help him with them anytime because I like training the dogs. I have a collie of my own called Jill. She's really good at rounding up the sheep we take on each year to graze the common.' His blue eyes shone with enthusiasm.

'The cows bring in the regular money for us,' Ranald said, 'and I suppose it will be the same over at your place?'

'That's what Dad keeps saying,' Jamie nodded, pulling a long face. 'He says I shall have to get used to milking every night and morning when I leave school next summer. Meg and I take turns just now but Meg enjoys cows and calves.'

'She's growing into a bonnie lassie your sister, with her long dark curls and sparkling green eyes,' Ranald remarked. 'She's like your mother.'

'Yes, she's all right is Meg,' Jamie said warmly. There was only a year between them and they had always been close. He sighed. 'Dad's always singing Meg's praises but she never gets big-headed and she's always willing to help, or to cover for me.' He grimaced. 'I never seem to please him and Meg hates quarrels. Oh look! There's two people waiting by the fence. Is that tall fellow your friend?'

'It is.'

As they drew nearer Jamie gasped in recognition. 'I know the little'un. He's a bit older than I am but he's in the same class at school. His name is George Mundy. Some of the lads call him Georgie Porgie.'

'Mmm, he looks a bit on the podgy side,' Ranald reflected. 'I hope he can keep up. He'd better not moan and want to go back if things get exciting. Bill reckons he's a bit of a weakling.' Jamie didn't answer. George was not one of his friends. He never went bird nesting and he rarely joined in any of the games. If he did, he always expected to win without putting in any effort and he complained to his older brother, Cyril, when he didn't get his own way. The family lived in the big house just outside Silverbeck village and rumour had it they were quite well off so Cyril was still at school, even though he was already fourteen and twice the size of George. He was idle and a bully, so Jamie and his friends were wary of the Mundy brothers.

As soon as Ranald's friend caught sight of them he grinned widely and set off up the hill in front of them. 'We should get a good view from the top,' he called. 'If we're lucky we shall see the red coats of the huntsmen and find which way they're heading.' It was fairly steep but not much worse than the common at home and Jamie was lithe and fit, so he could keep up fairly well with the two older boys. George was sturdier and not used to much physical effort — and he had eaten a huge lunch. He was soon out of breath and calling to his cousin Bill to wait for him and not to go so fast.

'For goodness' sake kid, you can't get lost up here even if you do fall behind. We're not going over the top — at least not unless we catch sight of the horses and the hounds in the valley bottom.'

'Make Sinclair wait for me then,' George said sulkily. 'I don't like being left on my own. I shall tell Auntie Betty on you.' Bill raised his eyes to heaven then grinned at his companions.

'Leave him to follow on,' he muttered. 'I knew he'd be a pest but my mother insisted I get him out of the house to give her a bit of peace from his whining. He's staying with us because his mother is having a baby. That will be a shock to him. He's used to being the baby in their family.'

'Whew, that's a big gap,' Ranald said. 'How old is he?'

'Thirteen, a bit older than me,' Jamie said.

Long before they reached the top of the hill, George was left behind to kick furiously at tufts of grass and generally feel sorry for himself.

Jamie was sorry they didn't get a closer look at the huntsmen but they caught a glimpse of them and heard the horn as they galloped over the hill on the opposite side of the valley.

'Oh well,' Ranald sighed, 'better luck next time but we'd better be getting back or Jamie and I will be in trouble. We both have cows to milk when we get home.'

'Don't you have cows to milk too?' Jamie asked Bill.

'No, we only keep a couple of house cows. We have a hill farm so we keep sheep. We have a small herd of beef cows and their calves as well though, and some pigs and hens of course.'

'And can you make a living without having milk to sell every day?' Jamie asked eagerly. Bill threw back his head and laughed aloud.

'We survive, and we're happy if that counts. Of course we're poor relations compared with Uncle Charles Mundy. He's married to Mam's sister and he's some kind of bigwig in the woollen mills, or at least he thinks he is. My aunt is all right. She and my mother have always been good friends. That's why she agreed to have George to stay for his holidays.' He lowered his voice. 'She agrees he's a spoiled brat.'

They had almost reached the grassy hump where George was sitting waiting for them and they could all see his scowl and the sulky pout of his thick lips. Jamie was not sorry when he and Ranald parted company with him and headed back to Blaketop.

As soon as he and his cousin entered the house, George whined to his aunt and uncle about the other three leaving him behind. They exchanged a brief smile and raised their eyes heavenward.

'Who were the other three?' his aunt asked, trying to show some interest in his grievance.

'One of them was cousin Bill's friend Ranald Kerr and he brought one of his relations. I know him. He's in my class at school but he went with them and left me. They all left me.' He scowled and looked sulky.

'Aah, that would be Drew Kerr's Scottish relatives who were visiting,' his aunt told her husband. 'I knew Annie Kerr had invited them over for Boxing Day. I'm so glad they were able to come. She really misses her Scottish relatives. I remember how happy Annie was when she heard the Sinclairs were moving down from Scotland to live at Moorend Farm. They had only been married the day before they arrived and the farmhouse at Moorend had been badly neglected so she was really excited about making them welcome and having them to stay at Blaketop for their first night of married life.'

'Aye, Annie is a kindly woman,' her husband said. He frowned thoughtfully. 'It couldn't have been when they were newly married though because I remember it was hay time, about July. The landlord let them into Moorend early. I'm sure Drew told me how busy they were at the time because they already had a young baby. I know they have quite a brood of children now.' Neither of them paid any attention to their nephew and his sullen moods so they were unaware of his malicious interest. He knew Jamie Sinclair was four months younger than him so that meant his birthday was at the beginning of June. He had a feeling his aunt and uncle considered there was something strange about that but he couldn't work out the significance and he was too lazy to rack his brains, even when he was at school. He put it out of his mind and concentrated on his grievances, hoping his aunt would give him one of the chocolates from the big box on the dining room table. His mother always gave him a sweet, or some other treat, to help him forget his tales of woe.

At Braeside, Maggie was enjoying being married to Joe, sharing their new home together and they had decided to celebrate the festive season in their own house. James Sinclair and Jim had agreed to join them for their Christmas midday meal and they had invited Joe's father to stay over Christmas and New Year. Bert was fiercely independent and he was keeping in good health, but he agreed to spend two nights with them over Christmas. As things turned out he enjoyed their company and Maggie's cooking so much he asked to stay with them until New Year's Day, when the rest of his family were coming to Braeside for the New Year celebrations. He would go home to Locheagle with them. Maggie was delighted by his change of plans and warmed by his praise. A few days after Christmas, Joe and Bert were picking Brussels sprouts in the garden and Maggie was standing at the kitchen window preparing lunch, when she heard the sound of hooves. A chestnut pony came into view ridden by a young girl. They stopped at the garden gate. Maggie dried her hands and went out to ask if the young rider was lost.

'Oh no, I wanted to come to Braeside. Grandfather said I might like to ride this way to give my new pony some exercise. He wondered if you had finished building your house and if it looks nice.'

'And who is your grandfather?' Maggie asked with a smile. 'And what is your name?'

'I am so sorry. I should have told you my name,' the child said, looking contrite. 'I am called Catherine but my brother always called me Rina and I like that better so my friends call me that too, and Grandfather of course.' She gave a mischievous grin. 'I think he calls me that because he knows I hate it when my parents call me Catherine.'

'I see,' Maggie said bemused by her young visitor. 'Why is your grandfather interested in Braeside?' The light dimmed momentarily from the girl's face.

'Because he can't ride any more since he was ill so he has never seen how your house looks now you have finished it. I shall tell him it looks very fine. He told my father he was sure you would make a fine job when they quarrelled over it.'

'I-I see . . .' Maggie said as Joe and his father strolled over to see them, carrying the basket of sprouts. Rina slid from the pony's back and held out a small hand to the two men.

'How do you do? My name is Rina Capel. I came to see your house so I can tell my grandfather how good it looks. He will be very pleased to know.'

'That is a fine big pony you have there,' Bert Greig said, his blue eyes twinkling. He liked the girl's wide smile and mischievous face. Her breeches looked a bit baggy, as though they didn't belong to her.

'My grandfather bought Duke for me for Christmas. He said I was too big to ride Dolly any longer. He says she is getting old, like him. I've had her for ever and I love Dolly so I didn't want any other pony. My father says she should be put away but Grandfather has promised she can stay in the paddock where he can see her every day and he will not let anyone take her away or harm her. He walks to the gate every day now he is getting better and he feeds her two sugar lumps.'

'So now you're riding this big fellow?' Joe said. 'Would you like to tie him to the post and come for a closer look at the house and garden?'

'Oh yes please, if you don't mind. Grandfather said I must not be nosey or cheeky.' She grinned up at Joe as he held open the garden gate. He grinned down at her, finding her smile infectious and quite delightful. But when she was standing next to Maggie, who was smoothing down her spotless white apron, she looked up anxiously, then down at her breeches. Her teeth were white and square and she fixed them on her lower lip. 'Perhaps I should not have come when I am wearing breeches. They are my brother's old ones. Mama does not approve so

I keep them at Grandfather's. I change out of my dress at his house. He keeps a wee room specially for me. He did buy me a smart side saddle when he bought Duke because he said it would keep Mama happier but he knows I like to ride astride without a saddle. He taught me to ride as soon as I could walk. He said Mary Queen of Scots was an excellent horse rider and he wanted me to be the same.' She paused for breath.

'Well, we don't mind your breeches, lassie,' Bert assured her.

'Would you like a drink of lemonade and a biscuit?' Maggie asked diffidently, unsure whether she should be entertaining the granddaughter of Sir Reginald Capel of Stavondale in her humble home. She never thought of the man as her own father.

'Yes please, that is if you will excuse me not going further than the kitchen when I am in my boots and breeches. Father would whip me if he knew I had come at all and especially dressed like a boy.'

'Oh, surely he would not whip you, Miss Capel,' Maggie said, her soft heart instantly captured and protocol forgotten. Maggie had been making butterscotch toffee and she had set the tin on the table to cool, for she had discovered Joe and his father enjoyed it as much as her young nieces and nephews. Joe liked a few pieces to eat on his train journey to and from work each day. She saw her young guest eying it.

'Do you like butterscotch toffee, Miss Capel?'

'Oh please don't call me that, Mrs Greig. It makes me think I'm back at school.' She pulled a face. 'I hate having to live away at school. When we had a nanny she used to make toffee for us if we had been good. I love it.'

'Then I shall break some pieces and wrap them in paper for you to eat on your ride home.'

'Thank you. The shortbread is lovely too.'

'Have another piece then, lassie,' Joe said. 'Maggie willna mind. She's a fine cook and she has a kind heart.' Rina looked at him and decided he meant it, so she helped herself to another triangular biscuit.

'Do you have any animals here or are they only at Bonnybrae Farm? Grandfather said all the Braeside land had been added to the Bonnybrae land so . . .'

'We have some hens and we have pigs in all three pigsties at present,' Joe said. 'One of them had twelve baby pigs last week.'

'Baby pigs! Oh my! Will you take me to see them? Please?'

'If you like, but you may find them a bit smelly. Pigs are clean animals really but they have to make their mess somewhere — they make it in their own small yard so they can keep their beds clean and dry inside.'

'Yes, I remember that. Grandfather used to take me with him to Home Farm to see all the animals. Then Mama insisted I must go away to school and learn to be a lady and I'm not allowed to go near Home Farm now.' She drank up her lemonade and brushed the biscuit crumbs from her mouth, then grinned up at Maggie.

'That was — it was . . .' she licked her lips with the tip of her pink tongue, 'delicious. May I come to see you again when I am on holiday from school? Duke needs more exercise than Dolly did. Grandfather says he will ask Ernest from the stables to exercise him when I am away but Father says he had no business to use Ernest for such tasks. Grandfather wishes I was old enough to ride round all the farms and tell him what the farmers are doing. I went with him sometimes before they sent me away to school. Some of the farmer's wives made tea and scones for us. Father was furious when I asked if I could go round the farms with him.'

Joe took her to see the litter of pigs and his heart warmed when she slipped her small hand into his and tiptoed after him, keeping to the side of the little pen where it was cleanest. 'I will not make a noise,' she whispered before they ducked low to get through the small opening into the inner pen. The sow lay on her side, grunting softly in encouragement, while all the piglets scrambled over each other to cling to their teat and suckle. Joe glanced down at Rina's wrapt expression. Her eyes were round with excitement and her lips formed an 'O'. Joe thought she might have stayed indefinitely but he considered they had detained her long enough so he drew her outside again.

Maggie, Joe and Bert all accompanied her to the garden gate. Before she mounted she carefully unwrapped the toffee Maggie had given her and selected a small piece for the pony, holding it out for him on the palm of her hand, then she put a larger piece in her own mouth, gave them a lopsided grin and leapt onto the pony's back with her bottom in the air until she managed to haul herself over and get her other leg astride. She turned to wave as she cantered away.

'Well, that may not be the ladylike way to mount her horse,' Bert chuckled, 'but she's a game wee lassie.'

'Mmm, I think her mother might have a hard job making her into a lady,' Joe said. 'If you ask me, she is a born tomboy and it sounds as though her grandfather encourages her escapades. I enjoyed her visit.'

'So did I. She's so innocent and natural, but I think the poor bairn must be a bit lonely,' Maggie said. 'I didn't think we should be asking a member of the laird's family in our house but she seemed pleased to come in. I ought to have taken her through to the parlour but she insisted on staying in the kitchen.'

'Have you ever met her brother?' Bert asked.

'We see the family at the kirk sometimes but the boy is at school in Edinburgh too. He is the eldest. His name is Jonathan, I think. I doubt if he will dare disobey his parents the way Miss Rina does,' Maggie added with a smile. The child's chatter, her honesty and openness had been enchanting.

None of them were surprised when Rina visited Braeside several more times during her Christmas holidays and she always wanted to see the little pigs. On her first return visit, she brought a letter from her grandfather to Maggie and Joe.

He thanked them for making his granddaughter welcome and for giving her so much pleasure, especially now that he was unable to take her round the estate himself. He said he was pleased to hear Braeside had turned out well for them and he wished them many years of happiness together. Both Joe and Maggie were delighted to receive his letter.

CHAPTER ELEVEN

Spring arrived and everyone at Bonnybrae was busy with lambing, in addition to the usual milking and dairy work and the wearying task of ploughing.

Back at Moorend, Jamie was approaching his last term at school. He was top of his class and was expected to get a good leaving certificate and maybe one or two of the special prizes, especially the one for nature study. He wondered how he would get on with his father when he had to work all day on the farm with him, Tom and Cliff, although he looked forward to tending the horses and learning to plough. He longed to have more time to spend with Jill. Even his father said she was shaping up to be one of the best working collies he had seen in a long time. She was a granddaughter of Queenie, the collie his parents had brought with them from Scotland. Until he was 5 years old and started school, Queenie had been his constant guardian and companion. In private, he had cried when she died.

Recently his father had mentioned there was an extra good dog belonging to a breeder who lived about twenty miles away. 'He would make a good mate for Jill when she is ready but his owner charges a hefty fee. If you work hard when you leave school we'll see what we can do about taking her there, then maybe you can start breeding and training your own sheep dogs like your Grandfather Sinclair did when he was younger.'

A couple of weeks before the Easter holidays, all the children in Jamie and Meg's class were asked to choose one of four poems and learn it by heart ready to recite it to the younger children in Miss Edgar's class on the last day of school. This was John and Allan's class. Jamie chose 'A Boy's Song' by James Hogg, because he knew the man had been a Scottish shepherd. Meg was torn between the poem about daffodils by William Wordsworth and 'The Lamb' by William Blake. The fourth choice was 'Meg Merrilies' by John Keats. No one, least of all Mr Thorpe, their teacher, could have foreseen the trouble and the ensuing consequences this assignment would cause.

Meg loved poetry and she learned both poems but she settled on 'The Lamb' as her choice because it reminded her of her visit to Scotland and her grandfather's lambs. It was the shortest of the poems but even during the first practice, Meg said it perfectly with a sincerity and meaning in her clear, sweet voice. Mr Thorpe did not give praise easily but he was touched by Meg's recitation and he praised her generously. Two of the older girls who were Jamie's age had elected to learn 'Meg Merrilies'. They were jealous of Meg's performance, especially when she was a year younger than them. They gave her no peace, morning, noon or after school. They called her teacher's pet and told her she was like Meg the gypsy woman and she must be related to the gypsies when she had such dark hair while her three brothers all had fair or ginger hair. They jeered and made up stories about her father being one of the gypsies from the common.

'My dad says they're always hanging about your farm. I'll bet you don't know which one is your dad.' Meg was dismayed and hurt by their malicious teasing. She had the sweetest nature and had never encountered nastiness before. She was good with the younger children, often helping them with their coats and buttons and woollen gloves in the winter.

Miss Edgar had remarked several times that she would make a good teacher herself one day; the little ones all liked her and ran to her if they were in trouble. Meg couldn't understand the two older girls being so horrid and claiming her beloved father couldn't possibly be her real dad. Meg began to hate her long, dark curls. When Jamie found her sobbing after the girls had taken her aside, pulled her hair and stolen her hair ribbon, she confided in him about them calling her 'old Meg the gypsy'.

'They say I am the brat of one of the gypsies from the common.'

'You go on home with Allan and John. I'll catch you up,' Jamie said. 'I'll not let them run after you.' Meg did as he bid, glad to get away from the group which had gathered.

'And what d'yer think you can do?' one of the girls jeered, calling for the rest of them to join in and back her up. 'Your sister is a gypo. She's just like old Meg in the poem. Did your mother call her after that old woman? She doesn't look like you, or your brothers. Her hair is black like a gypsy's.'

'You all know she is not a gypsy. Her hair is like our mam's. It's better than your mousey brown colour. You're just jealous because Mr Thorpe praised Meg for saying her poem so well.'

''Course we're not jealous. She's Mr Thorpe's little pet. Anyway, it's nothing to do with you and you daren't hit us because we're lasses — you'll get the cane if you hit us.'

'I can tell Mr Thorpe how horrid you've been and that you have stolen Meg's hair ribbon, then he'll keep you in after school. He might cane you too for stealing.'

'Here, take 'er bloody ribbon,' one of the girls shouted and threw the red satin ribbon in the dust. She put her foot on it when Jamie bent to retrieve it but the next thing he knew, he was slumped in the dirt himself after a hefty thump in the back. Two or three boys had joined the girls and they all began to laugh. Jamie turned his head and saw at once it had been George Mundy who had pushed him so hard and sent him sprawling. There was nothing to say you couldn't hit boys. Jamie pushed aside the girl's foot and put Meg's dirty ribbon in his pocket. The next moment he had sprung to his feet and punched George Mundy in the nose. George howled loudly. He clapped a hand to his face and when he saw blood trickling onto his fingers, he shrieked in panic.

'He tried to kill me! Sinclair attacked me. Cyril! Cyril, where are you? You've got to pay him back. I'm bleeding.' Although Cyril had left school at Christmas he was still not working in the mill, as he had told everyone he was going to do. He usually hung around the school at closing time but he never came into the school yard. They were outside the yard now and most of the other children were on their way home, unaware of the squabble. Only the two bullying girls remained with George Mundy and his so-called friends, two younger boys who lived in the same part of Silverbeck village as the Mundys and were afraid to disagree with George and his brother. Jamie turned away in disgust at George whining for his big brother. He was the one who had knocked him over and he didn't like retaliation. He felt someone grab his shoulder and spin him round.

'What's this? You knocking my brother about?' Cyril confronted Jamie. He was built like Cliff Barnes except Cliff was solid and strong, while Cyril was broad and flabby. Even so he was considerably taller and heavier than Jamie, whose own friends would be well on their way home by now, unaware of the excitement or they would have stayed to watch him deal with George. Cyril was another matter. Apart from his size, they all knew he was a dirty fighter and spiteful.

'Your brother knocked me over,' Jamie said and would have kept on walking but Cyril lashed out and slapped Jamie's head then grabbed him and shook him like a rabbit, making his teeth chatter with the force. Furious at Cyril's unwarranted interference, Jamie lashed out with his feet and his stout leather boots proved a good weapon against Cyril's shins. He yelped in pain and slackened his grip. Jamie twisted free. He knew Cyril would hit him again so he decided to get in first. He took a few steps back then ran at Cyril, butting him in his fat belly with all the force he could command. To his surprise, large though he was, Cyril Mundy folded like a deflated balloon and landed on the grass. As soon as he could get his breath, he swore at Jamie.

'You're a bastard, Sinclair! Is your name really Sinclair? Your mother had you before she ever came to Yorkshire. I'll bet she was a whore before she married your father, if they are married! I'll bet you don't know who your father is. Auntie Betty said he's just a dirty little bastard, didn't she, George?' Jamie froze at the word 'bastard'. A picture of the old woman who looked like a witch flashed clearly in his mind. He thought he had forgotten her. They had told him she was his grandmother but she had said he was not a Sinclair. He was barely aware of Cyril hauling himself to his feet until he felt his fist hit him in the eye. For a moment he saw stars. Then he clenched his own fists and went for Cyril with all his strength. The big fellow was taken by surprise. No one attacked him! One punch landed under Cyril's jowls temporarily knocking his head back and catching him on his windpipe. He bent over coughing. Jamie kicked him hard on both legs then took to his heels and ran. He knew the Mundy brothers wouldn't dare attack him in the village. Jamie knew he would have a black eye and he wondered how he would explain that to his father. He could never tell his parents what Mundy had called him, or what he had said about his mother. It didn't matter whether it was true or not, it would be all over the school by tomorrow.

He walked quickly through the village until he saw Meg and his brothers in the distance, walking along the lane to Moorend. As she did every day, his own little collie dog, Jill, came to meet him before he reached the farmyard. She wagged her tail and held out a paw. He bent and hugged her, stroking her silky fur, glad to lay his stinging cheek against her head. They walked on together.

As they approached the house William, Emma and Tom were just coming out to start the milking after enjoying a cup of tea and scones.

'Jamie! Whatever has happened to you?' asked his father. 'Dear laddie, your face is bleeding . . .' It was only then Jamie remembered George Mundy had thrown a sharp stone at him at the same time as Cyril called him a bastard. He had been too stunned by the kind of abuse Cyril was shouting at him to pay attention to the blow. He lifted his hand to his face now and found he was bleeding a little.

'It's nothing,' he mumbled, wanting to push past them and escape, but it was not so easy. His father gripped his chin and lifted up his head.

'You're going to have a nasty black eye. You must have been fighting instead of getting yourself home from school. What happened?'

'Leave it for now, William,' his mother said, smoothing his hair back from the cut on his temple. 'Let me clean that cut and see what I can do.'

'Don't be soft with him, Emma. He'll be a man soon. He should be getting himself home to do his work after school instead of . . .'

'Don't blame Jamie, Dad,' Meg cried, rushing back out of the house at the sound of her father's angry words. 'He was defending me.' Jamie summoned a crooked smile for Meg and held out her ribbon. 'I got it back but it doesn't look very good now.'

'Och, there's nothing a good wash and iron willna cure,' Emma said briskly, reverting to her Scottish twang as she did when she was upset or excited. She took the ribbon herself. 'Surely you didn't get a black eye fighting over a hair ribbon, Jamie?'

'Oh, Jamie . . .' Meg's voice trembled when she looked more closely at her brother with his dirty trousers and bleeding face. 'Surely those horrid girls didn't do that to you?' she asked incredulously.

'What girls and what were they doing to you, Meg, that Jamie needed to defend you?' Emma asked, trying to draw Jamie into the house with her. William blocked their path, frowning. He knew Jamie was far from soft.

'It wasna girls who gave you a black eye though, was it?'

'No, it was Mundy and his brother. They're always looking for trouble.'

'B-but it was the girls who started it,' Meg said, her mouth trembling. 'They said I look like the gypsies on the common and one of them must be m-my f-father.'

'I'm your father, Meg, you know that.' William put an arm around her thin shoulders and drew her to him. 'Whatever made them say such a thing?'

'They said it's because I have black hair and my brothers are fair so I must be a gypsy and I don't know who my father is.'

'That's ridiculous,' Emma said indignantly. 'Your hair is the same colour as mine and Uncle Joe's and Uncle Richard's. You have lovely hair, Meg.'

'They only said it because they're jealous of Meg,' Jamie said. 'We all had to learn a poem and when Meg said hers, Mr Thorpe said she had done it beautifully and she deserved to get the poetry prize at the end of the year, even though she's a year younger than the two who were bullying her.' He turned away to go into the house and avoid his father's keen scrutiny.

'Just a minute,' William said sternly. 'What has all this to do with the lads who hit you?'

'I told you. The girls had pulled Meg's hair and — and made her cry and they took her ribbon. I told them to stop chasing her and to give back the ribbon. One of them threw it on the floor and stood on it. I bent to pick it up and George Mundy came up behind and sent me sprawling in the muck so I got up and punched him in the nose and made it bleed. He whined like a baby. Oh I know, I know, you keep saying we shouldn't fight, Dad, but he deserved it.'

'He whined like a baby but he still gave you a black eye?'

'No, he did not! That was his big brother, Cyril Mundy . . .' Jamie's face paled as he remembered the words Cyril Mundy had called after him. He could never repeat them to his parents, especially his mother. His beloved mam had never been what Cyril had called her.

'Did you hear what I said?' William said sharply, grasping his shoulder. 'I'm telling you, you will have to say you're sorry to the Mundy lads tomorrow, and make it a good apology in front of Mr Thorpe.'

'No! I will not. Mr Thorpe will cane me for fighting, even though it was out of the school yard, but he never canes George Mundy.'

'Of course he doesn't. That's what I'm telling you. Mr Mundy, their father, is one of the school governors, or some such official. He could have you put out of school and then you'll have a black mark on your character for life, instead of the fine leaving report your mother and I are expecting. I mean it, James Sinclair. You must apologise tomorrow first thing.'

Jamie pulled away and went into the house with his head bent. Meg and his mother trailed after him while William went to start the milking.

'James Sinclair' his father had called him. He called him James when he was annoyed and stern with him, but surely he wouldn't have called him Sinclair if he were a bastard? If he were not his son? He shuddered. If William Sinclair was not his father, then who was he? He could guess at the hints and rumours George Mundy would spread around the school tomorrow. They would be all over the village when the children went home. Deep down Jamie sensed there had always been a reservation between him and his father, which was not there with his brothers or Meg or Marie. There was something his parents had never told him, but what? The old woman who was supposed to be his grandmother had known something. She had said he was not a Sinclair. But how had the Mundy family got such a rumour? He didn't even know their aunt. It upset him to think his parents were keeping secrets from him and strangers knew what they were.

He changed out of his school clothes and shook his shorts and jersey to get rid of the dust. He placed them neatly over a chair as his mother had instructed many times so that they were ready for morning and another day at school. He didn't care about the caning but he shivered at the prospect of the jeering and tales and rumours. If only he could be certain there was no truth in Mundy's tales. One thing was for sure; he would not apologise to George Mundy whatever his father said, not even if Mr Thorpe caned him until he couldn't sit down. His stomach churned. Could Mr Mundy get him expelled from school for giving his son a bloody nose? He was due to leave after the summer term anyway because he would be fourteen in June and ready for work but he didn't want to leave with a black mark against his character. He had expected to get a good leaving certificate, maybe the prize for nature study and perhaps the one for arithmetic too. These thoughts went round and round in his head as he did the tasks he and Meg, Allan and John all had to do after school. One of his jobs was to help Cliff Barnes feed and groom the horses. Cliff was good at grooming but his brain did not always remember how much feed each of the horses should have. Jamie was secretly pleased that his father trusted him to remember and to supervise the feeding without upsetting Cliff when he got it wrong. He usually made a joke of any mistakes and he and Cliff would laugh together. His father had explained what a cruel childhood Cliff had endured at the hands of his stepfather, so he was always patient and he never made fun of the big man.

When that was done he had to go to the common, count the sheep and see if any were lame or needing attention. Over the years his father had gradually taken on more sheep twice a year to graze the common because none of the other farmers around Silverbeck seemed to want the bother of herding sheep or cattle on the unfenced land, although they could all claim a share in the grazing if they wanted it. Garridan said the grass on the common was fresher and greener each year since his father had come to Moorend. The gypsies also grazed their few horses and goats there but they always kept them closer to the site where they camped. Lord Hanley didn't complain, so long as they did not steal or cause trouble with the local people.

Jamie whistled for Jill and together they set off. He enjoyed this more than anything else and he loved Jill. She was getting better and better every day at obeying his commands and sensing what he needed almost before he knew himself. Even his father was impressed with them both and the way they worked together. Once, when he was in an extra good mood, he had said when Jamie left school they might keep some sheep of their own for breeding if he could rent more acres of land with a proper lease, if it was fairly near Moorend land. Jamie dreamed about this but even he knew land to rent was scarce; none of the local farmers were likely to give up their farms, so it was just a big 'if' at some distant time, rather than a promise.

Jamie could not eat his supper with his usual appetite. Both Emma and Polly asked if he had a bad headache and were sympathetic about his eye, which seemed to be getting darker by the minute, although the cut on his temple had stopped bleeding and didn't look so bad after it had been washed. His father was brusque, his tone uncompromising.

'Remember and apologise to the Mundy lad as soon as you get to school. I don't want to hear of you being banned for being a ruffian.' The words rang in Jamie's head as he went upstairs to the bedroom he shared with Allan, John and Peter. They were already sound asleep. Jamie was tired too but his father's admonition echoed in his head as the events of the day recurred in his troubled dreams. Sometime in the night he wakened and the thought was as clear as if he had heard it spoken, or read it in a book. If he did not go to school the authorities — whoever they were — could not ban him. If he was not there he could not apologise to George Mundy and neither could Mr Thorpe cane him unjustly, for it was the injustice that hurt Jamie's pride, far more than the pain of the cane. Sometime later he heard his parents going downstairs, he heard Polly raking out the fire and the rumble of Cliff's heavy footsteps as they all went outside to start the milking and the rest of the morning feeds and cleaning.

Where could he go if he didn't go to school? He could spend all day with the gypsies and they would not tell tales, but what after that? He couldn't live with them. He remembered Grandfather Greig the day he and Uncle Joe went to catch the train back to Scotland. They had both said he would always be welcome to visit. But Grandfather Greig was an old man and he could not afford to keep him until he could find work. Grandfather Sinclair had said he could go and help him herd his sheep and train his dogs any time he liked. Had he meant it? Yes, Jamie was sure he had spoken the truth, and the old witch they had told him was his grandmother was dead now. But how was he to get to Scotland? He had no money to pay his fare. It never occurred to him to steal the money, or even to borrow it without permission, for all he knew his mother kept her egg money in the tin box.

He had only one possession that truly belonged to him. He felt sick at the thought. It would surely be better to take Mr Thorpe's punishment and leave school in disgrace, and even to suffer the malicious stories about his mother, than to part with his beloved Jill, his faithful, trusting little collie.

He could not sleep again, or even rest. He climbed out of bed and washed his face quickly and quietly so he did not disturb his brothers. Even as he did this and dressed himself, the thoughts were crystalizing in his mind. He knew Garridan would take good care of Jill. He had often said he would like a dog like her if Jamie ever got another to train. Would he buy her from him and give him money, though? Jamie knew the gypsies preferred to barter rather than part with their cash, but he needed coins to buy a train ticket. He didn't even know how much but he did know there was a train that left before the school bell rang. Even as the thoughts were going round in his head, he was stripping off his pillowcase and stuffing his working clothes in it, his pyjamas and socks, his best jersey. He tied the bundle up as small as he could make it and went out to the landing so that he could open the window and throw it into the garden without wakening his brothers.

Quickly, he dressed in his school clothes. Downstairs he pulled on his boots and laced them firmly then took his coat from the peg in the hall. He felt too sick to eat but he went into the pantry and poured himself a large cup of buttermilk. There was the end of a loaf in the bread bin as well as whole loaves and scones. He took the piece and spread on a lump of butter, then wrapped it in a piece of muslin. Outside he called softly for Jill. She ran to his side immediately and he caressed her soft head and crouched down. How could he leave her? Tears started to his eyes but he brushed them away impatiently. Jill looked up at him, her gentle brown eyes trusting. How could he even think of letting her go, even to Garridan? How else could he get away from school? His thoughts were in such turmoil he almost forgot his spare clothes lying in the garden and he had to turn back for them.

A few of the gypsies were up and about, including Garridan.

'You're about early this morning,' he called as he came to meet Jamie. 'Is something wrong? Ah, I see you have been in trouble,' he said as he drew nearer and saw Jamie's black eye. It looked worse this morning so there was no denying it. 'You been fighting, eh?'

'Yes I have, but Dad says I must apologise even though it was Mundy who started it.' He couldn't tell Garridan how upset Meg had been because they said her father was a gypsy, nor would he repeat what Cyril Mundy had called his mother. He was not sure exactly what the word meant but he did know it was the worst insult anyone could call a woman and Mundy clearly thought it meant his father could be any man, anywhere. He shuddered. Garridan could see there was something worse than a fight on his mind.

'All our gypsy children get into fights when we send them to schools on our travels, except when we spend the winter in Ireland. That is where we get most of our learning.'

'I don't mind fights. I would do it again. The Mundy brothers deserve a beating.' His lean jaw clenched. 'I'm not bothered about the caning we get for fighting either but Dad says Mr Mundy is some kind of official at the school and he will be ashamed of me if they stop me going to school for being a hooligan. He says it will be a black mark on my character for the rest of my life. If Mr Rowbottom, the land agent, heard I have been sent away from school with a blemish on my character and if — if . . . well if he hears other things, he might hold it against me. I might never get in line for a farm tenancy when I'm old enough.'

'Surely they would never prevent you finishing your education!' Garridan said indignantly.

'They can't do anything if I leave school first, can they? So that's what I want to do. I want to go to Scotland to my grandfather. I need you to keep it a secret, Garridan. I-I want you to — to b-buy Jill to give me enough money to buy the train ticket, and I need to hurry to get the train. Will you promise you will n-never sell her to anybody else? Will you look after her and — and l-love her like I do?' He bent down and laid his cheek next to Jill's silky head. She sensed there was something wrong and she leaned into him as though to comfort him. Garridan would have argued but he knew now how seriously Jamie was taking this trouble in his young life. Not only was he running away from his family, he was leaving his most treasured possession. He could see Jamie was near to tears. He knew how ashamed he would be if anyone saw them.

'I don't have a lot of cash, Jamie, but I expect I should have enough to buy you a train ticket and I promise I will care for Jill as well as you do yourself. You know I've always wanted her, or one like her.'

'I kn-know.' Jamie gulped. 'I haven't fed her. I thought she would settle better if you feed her.'

'Right then. There's not much time if you want to catch the early train north. I shall need to tie her up or she will run after us, or back to Moorend.'

'I know.'

'Wait here then,' Garridan said gently and took Jill's lead in his hand. The little collie knew him but for all that, she kept looking back to Jamie and tugging on her collar. Jamie couldn't watch. He had turned his back and was walking slowly away. He knew Garridan would catch him up as soon as he could.

Garridan not only caught him up, he came riding one of the horses. It was part Shire and part hunter, so it was lighter and faster that the two heavy horses Garridan kept for pulling his caravan and trailer.

'Can you jump up behind me?' Garridan said cheerfully. 'It will be quicker this way and we can go across country, straight to Wakefield. You'll not be wanting to run into anyone waiting for the milk train at Silverbeck.'

'Gosh no! I hadn't thought of that.' He shivered. 'But I didn't mean to put you to any trouble, Garridan.'

'It's no trouble to help a friend. I want to make sure we have enough money for your ticket, and to give you a ten-shilling note to keep in your pocket in case anything goes wrong.'

'Thank you.' Jamie's voice was husky and he was glad he was behind so Garridan could not see him brushing away the unmanly tears that kept gathering.

'Didn't your father say there was an extra good dog he would have liked to mate with Jill when she's old enough to have puppies?' Garridan asked.

'Yes, he did, but he belongs to a shepherd and he charges a lot of money for a mating because he knows his dog is a good breeder.'

'Where does he live?'

'I don't know but he's at least twenty miles north of Moorend. I don't know what the name of the farm is where he works.'

'Do you know the shepherd's name?'

'Yes, he's called Bentham. Ed Bentham, I think.'

'Good.' Garridan nodded. He smiled to himself. There were ways of finding out where people lived when you were used to roaming the countryside and taking your home with you. There were ways of lending nature a hand too when a bitch was on heat and there was a good dog not far away. Surely he and Jamie would meet again someday. One way or another, he would repay him. Garridan knew Jamie had trusted him today more than he trusted anyone else in his small world. He also knew that he and Jill would have to make themselves scarce for a few days if he were to avoid answering questions. William Sinclair might be stern, and sometimes impatient, with his eldest son but Garridan was sure Mrs Sinclair loved all her children. They would search for Jamie until they knew he was safe. He hoped the lad's faith in his Scottish relatives would not be misplaced and he prayed William Sinclair would not hold it against him for helping his son, if he ever found out.

CHAPTER TWELVE

As soon as the milking was finished, Emma always hurried into the house to make sure her four eldest got a good breakfast and were ready for school on time. Polly stayed in the dairy to wash the buckets and milk cooler while William measured milk into a gallon can for the house, then measured and noted the quantity in each churn before sealing it ready to take to the station and get it on the train to the creamery. It was always a rush to get everything done on time in the mornings.

They were all supping their porridge with relish when Emma noticed Jamie had not put in an appearance yet.

'Allan, will you shout upstairs and tell him to hurry? He'll be late for school.'

'I think he's already gone to school. His school trousers and jumper were gone when we were getting dressed, weren't they John?' His younger brother nodded.

'Ah, he's a good lad,' William said with satisfaction. 'I could see he didn't like the idea of apologising to those Mundy lads, but if you have to do something you don't like it's best to get it over and done, then you can enjoy the rest of the day. Remember that, you two laddies.'

'He'll not enjoy the rest of the day,' Meg said unhappily. 'Mr Thorpe will cane him for fighting, especially when he sees his black eye. It was all because of me but it was nothing to do with George Mundy. He never gets caned. It's not fair.'

'Life is often not fair, lassie,' William said, 'but we have to make the best of it. I don't know exactly what Mr Mundy has to do with the running of the school but Joe Wright says he has a lot of influence in this area and the way things are run. Anyway it's better not to get on the wrong side of people like that.' William finished his breakfast and pushed back his chair. 'I'd better get off to the station if I'm to catch the milk train. Are you finished, Cliff? I need a hand to load the churns into the cart.' Cliff did the same thing every morning but he always needed reminding of their routine.

Meg was dismayed when she arrived at school and discovered Jamie was not there. Where could he be? Was he hiding at home in the barn, or somewhere, until it was too late to come? All day she was on edge. She knew their father would be furious when he discovered Jamie had not been to school, or said he was sorry to George Mundy. You couldn't see any marks on him this morning. Meg was usually gentle but she wished Jamie had hit him so hard he had broken his nose and not just made it bleed. It would have served him right. For once the two girls who picked on her were quiet and minding their own business. They were in awe of Jamie Sinclair.

Garridan tethered his horse outside the station, then went and bought the ticket himself. He handed it to Jamie along with the promised ten-shilling note. Jamie had never had so much money in his life.

'I-I'll pay you back, Garridan.'

'I reckon Jill has more than paid me back already. The man in the ticket office gave me a strange look. I reckon he recognizes us gypsies and he would be wondering why I was going on a train.' He grinned. 'If anybody enquires whether a young lad has bought a ticket today he can't say he's seen you, can he?'

'I never thought of that,' Jamie said. His stomach was churning and now the time had come, he wondered if he was doing the wrong thing. Supposing his grandfather hadn't meant what he said?

'This seems to be the train north just coming in, I think,' Garridan said uncertainly. 'Here's an apple to eat on the way. Does it take long to get to Scotland on the train?'

'It seemed to take forever when we came with Mam,' Jamie admitted. Garridan could see he was nervous and his emotions were raw.

'You'll be fine,' he said gruffly, but he saw Jamie safely into a carriage and slammed the door then disappeared from sight, knowing a prolonged farewell would only make things worse. He had known Jamie since he was a baby in his mother's arms and he had watched him grow and learn. The truth was he was fond of his young friend, more so than Garridan had realized until he saw the train drawing away with the lad on board.

Jamie sat tensely on the edge of his seat for most of the journey. He could not relax to enjoy the sights of the countryside flying by, not even when he saw young lambs with their mothers so close to the railway they seemed to be almost on the line, yet they lay sleeping, undisturbed by the noise and steam of the clattering train. When he and Meg had accompanied their mother, they had got off at the nearest station to Grandfather Greig's house at Locheagle. It was the only way he knew so that was the way he would have to go. He knew Uncle Joe travelled from a different station to his work since he had moved to Braeside but Jamie had no idea what it was called or how to get from there to Bonnybrae. His stomach rumbled as the miles sped by and he unwrapped the crust of bread he had brought. It was not as big as he had thought so he demolished it with speed. He did not possess a watch; he had no idea of the time and a little while later he ate the apple Garridan had provided, wishing he had taken time to eat a bowl of porridge before he left but Polly had only just set it on the rib to cook when he sneaked out of the door.

Exhausted with tension and walking from the station, he stumbled as he went up the path to his grandfather's cottage. Bert was just stirring from his afternoon nap, which he seemed to need most days now, but at least it kept him going. He couldn't believe his eyes when he saw the tall, slim laddie walking up his garden path. He went to the door and held it wide.

'Jamie? Can it really be you, Jamie?' He held out his arms and drew his grandson into them; amazement, pleasure and bewilderment vying with each other. 'Well come in, come into the hoose, ma laddie,' he said, ushering Jamie inside. The cottage was much as he remembered except that his grandmother no longer lay in the box bed beside the fire. Bert pushed the kettle over the hot coals.

'My, but 'tis grand tae see ye, laddie,' Bert said warmly. 'Ye must be hungry after that long journey and walking frae the station.' Julie had brought him a new baked loaf that morning; he lifted it out of the bread bin and set it on the board with a dish of butter. 'I canna offer ye any meat but I have a good piece of cheese.'

'Oh Grandfather,' Jamie's voice shook and he took a deep breath, striving for control. 'Just the bread and butter and a cup of tea will be very welcome. I-I'm famished now I see food.' He was indeed and Bert watched him slice a thick chunk of bread and butter it. It was demolished in no time. Bert poured them both a cup of hot, strong tea and kept on filling up Jamie's cup until most of the loaf and all the cheese had disappeared. That didn't worry Bert. He could go to the shop to get some more cheese and Julie would be bringing him some soda scones in the morning when she baked. Jamie was glad his grandfather had not bombarded him with questions but now that he had food inside him, he felt better and he knew he had to give an explanation for his unexpected arrival.

'Are they all well back home, Jamie? Your mother? Has she got over losing the baby?' Jamie had meant to tell them all he wanted to leave school and work for his living and would rather work with the sheep and the dogs at Bonnybrae than milk cows all the time. He had rehearsed it on the train but when he looked into Grandfather Greig's kind and honest face, his gentle blue eyes that seemed to look into his soul, the words came tumbling out of their own accord. He told him about the poetry and how well Meg had recited hers and earned exceptional praise from Mr Thorpe and incurred the malice and jealousy of two older girls.

'Aye, I like a wee bit of poetry myself, and so did Uncle Davy and your mother, but surely there was no need to take out their spite on wee Meg.'

'No there wasn't, and I told them so when they tugged her hair and stole her best red hair ribbon.' He went on to tell his grandfather about the Mundy boys joining in and their father being a school governor and how his father thought he should apologise to avoid getting a black mark on his leaving certificate, or worse, being banned from the school.

'I didn't care about all that, Grandfather, or about getting caned for fighting, b-but Cyril Mundy says I'm a — a bastard because my mother was not married when I was born and he says . . .' He heard his grandfather's indrawn breath but he went on, '. . . He says my father could be anybody and I'll never know whether I should be Sinclair or n-not.' He couldn't tell his grandfather they had called his mother a whore because she was his daughter and anyway, he was sure it wasn't true.

'Did you tell your mother and father what the laddies said?' Bert Greig asked slowly. He looked troubled but Jamie was too upset to notice as he recounted the things that had been going round and round in his own young and troubled mind.

'I don't know how the Mundys know these things about me but I know there's something they haven't told me because the old woman who was supposed to be my grandmother called me a bastard and she said I was not a Sinclair. It will be all over the school today and everybody will be whispering and sp-spreading rumours and by tomorrow it will be all over the village, so I thought it was better if I'm not there to bring worry to my mam. I know she is my mam, isn't she, Grandfather?' He looked up then and Bert saw the anxiety in his blue eyes, in spite of the conviction in his voice.

'She certainly is your mother, laddie, and I can tell ye for sure that William Sinclair is your father. He never had any doubts about that so neither should you. I had a letter from him once but I canna recall where we put it, a real nice letter it was, telling us he was your father.'

'Did you? Did you really have a letter, Grandfather?'

'I did. I expect your grandmother put it away in a safe place.'

'There is something though, I know there is. Some secret they haven't told me. Why did the old woman say I was not a Sinclair? Dad is always sterner with me than with the rest. He always has been. Anyway I'm not going back there. I shall be fourteen in June. All I want is to earn my living. I would like to work for Grandfather Sinclair if he'll have me, with the sheep and the d-dogs.' His voice shook as he remembered he had left his beloved Jill behind. 'I didn't know which station to get off to go to Bonnybrae so I came to find you first. I'm sorry if I'm a bother to you, Grandfather.'

'Eh laddie, ye're not a bother to me.' He gave him a big hug and kept his arms around him, holding him against his chest because his voice was gruff and he didn't want him to see the tears in his old eyes. 'I thought I might never see you again and here you are. I reckon ye're a brave laddie to find your way on such a long journey and all on your own.' He released him.

'Th-thank you,' Jamie said gratefully.

'I've plenty of room for ye to stay here if you want, and if ye're tired. It's another three miles further up the glen to Bonnybrae, but I expect ye'll remember that?'

'I do, but I shall not be able to sleep until I know whether Grandfather will give me work so that I can earn my keep.' He sounded young and uncertain and Bert felt a spurt of anger against William and Emma for letting the laddie get in such a state.

'Your Aunt Meg and Uncle Joe will be as pleased to see ye as I am. I'll bet Maggie will insist on keeping ye at their house when she sees ye. She should have been a mother herself. She's such a kind and loving woman. Come to think of it, your Uncle Jim might believe the angels have answered his prayers and sent ye to help him. His father — your Grandfather Sinclair — has taken ill. He had a very bad chill and it settled on his chest so the doctor warned him not to go up the hill or out in the cold wind, just when he's needed as the lambing is beginning. I reckon Jim will be glad o' a pair o' young legs and strong arms to help him round up the ewes and catch them and their lambs.'

'You really think so, Grandfather?'

'I'll bet my life on it, laddie. They will all be pleased to see ye.' Although privately, he wondered what Emma and William would have to say about it.

'Then if you don't mind, I ought to get on. I'm sorry I ate so much. I was very hungry.'

'Of course ye were and I'm pleased ye came to me. I'll set ye on the way to Bonnybrae if ye wait while I get my jacket and cap.'

Jamie lifted his pathetically small bundle and wandered slowly down the garden path, waiting for his grandfather to catch him up. He thought he could remember the way to Braeside where Uncle Joe and Aunt Maggie had built their new house but he was very tired, so he didn't want to get lost and walk extra miles.

They had gone just over a mile when they saw a horse and rider cantering across one of the fields. The rider waved to them. The hedge was not high and the horse jumped over effortlessly, landing on the track about a hundred yards in front of them. Jamie was surprised to see the rider was a young girl. She looked younger than his sister, Meg. She turned to greet them, bringing the horse to an obedient halt.

'Good afternoon, Mr Greig,' she called, her eyes sparkling. Her smile was wide and friendly. 'Are you on the way to Braeside?' she asked eagerly. 'May I come with you?'

'Good afternoon to you, Miss Rina.' Bert Greig answered her greeting with a twinkle in his blue eyes. He liked the laird's granddaughter very much each time they met. 'Don't tell me you are on holiday from that school of yours again?'

'I am,' she giggled. 'They give us longer holidays to make up for us having to live there during term.'

'You live at the school?' Jamie couldn't help the question which burst from his lips. He would hate that. The girl pulled a face.

'We go to Edinburgh so we have to board there. I would rather live at home and go to school here but Mother wants us out of the way.'

'Now Miss Rina, you know your parents just want to give you a good education,' Bert said with gentle reproof. 'All parents want what is best for their children,' he added, looking Jamie in the eye. 'This is my grandson, Jamie Sinclair. I am setting him on the way to Braeside to stay with his aunt and uncle.'

'You're going to stay with Mr and Mrs Greig? Oh lucky you! Mrs Greig makes the best butterscotch toffee in all the world.'

'Yes, I remember. She made some for us when we came to visit before.'

'If you're going there now, I could come with you and give you a ride if you can jump up behind me. Duke will not mind, will you boy?' She leaned forward and gave the pony a vigorous pat. 'I could pull him alongside that gate if you can get on from there? Would that be all right, Mr Greig?'

'It would suit me fine, lassie. It will save my old legs.' Before they parted he had to ask Jamie the question that had been troubling him since he arrived. 'Jamie, did ye . . . did ye tell your mother or Meg where ye were going today?'

'No.' Jamie flushed guiltily. 'I didn't want them to stop me.' He chewed his lower lip and looked uncertainly at his grandfather.

'All right, laddie. Give my regards to Maggie.' He waited until Jamie had mounted the horse behind Rina, then he handed him his bundle. 'I'll see ye soon. Everything will be fine.'

Jamie was weary so he was happy to ride behind Rina, as he had ridden behind Garridan at the beginning of his journey. He felt a little shy about holding onto her but when she spurred Duke into a canter, he put his arms round her middle and held on more firmly. She was soft and cuddly and he rather liked the feel of her. She was plumper than Meg, more like his younger sister, Marie. He often cuddled her when she needed comforting but somehow, cuddling Rina was different and very satisfying.

'What is your surname?' he asked. 'Do you live near Braeside?'

'I'm Catherine Capel but my friends call me Rina. I live a few miles over there.' She waved a hand vaguely across the fields but she did not say she lived at Stavondale Tower, nor did she say her grandfather was Sir Reginald Capel of Stavondale, his grandfather's landlord.

Bert Greig watched them ride away for a moment then he turned and walked back the way they had come, glad it was downhill. Even so he didn't think he would reach the village before the post office closed but if he could catch Mrs Dickson, she would send a telegram to get to Moorend first thing in the morning. He would simply say that Jamie had arrived safely. That would not give any cause for extra gossip at the other end but it would let Emma and William know Jamie was all right. He was certain they would be worried sick when Meg got home from school and they realized he was missing.

Emma was indeed worried when Meg reported that Jamie had not been to school at all. Where could he have been hiding all day? He had not waited for the sandwiches she always gave them for their dinner. Had he taken anything from the pantry? He had not even waited for his breakfast, she remembered.

William was furious. 'I can't believe any son of mine could be such a coward that he's afraid to go to school and take a caning as punishment for bad behaviour.'

'Jamie isn't a coward, Dad,' Meg protested, near to tears. 'He's had the cane lots of times and he never cries like George Mundy did the one time Mr Thorpe caned him.'

Polly loved all the children but she had a special place in her heart for Jamie, because he had been her first charge when she came to Moorend Farm as a 14-year-old.

'It is the Mundy lads who are bullies and cowards,' she said fiercely. 'I've heard Uncle Joe and Aunt Ivy say they both deserve a good belting but nobody at Silverbeck dare tell them off in case they get into trouble from Mr Mundy, especially if they live in one of his houses — and he owns half the village at the far end.'

'Well, Jamie had better get himself back here and get his jobs done,' William said grimly, 'or it will be my belt he'll feel. We had better get on with the milking instead of wasting time waiting for him to get home.'

'He may not have gone far,' Polly said. 'He could be hiding in the loft until he hears the cows being milked.'

'Yes, he must be somewhere like that,' Emma said with a note of relief. 'After all, he will not know what time it is.'

'No, I suppose not,' William said, frowning, 'but I'm disappointed in him staying away from school on account of a bit of a fight.'

Meg waited while her father went outside then she tugged at her mother's hand. 'Jamie is not afraid of the cane, or of any of the lads. Cyril Mundy was there again, outside the school gates. They were saying all sorts of nasty things and jeering and spreading tales about Jamie. They — they asked me "Where is your bastard brother today?" When I didn't answer they shouted it more than once and then they said, "If he really is your brother". Some of the others laughed and repeated what they were saying. What is a bastard, Mam?' She didn't notice how white her mother's face had turned.

'It — it's a nasty swear word,' Emma said, but her voice was choked. Had they used it instead of calling Jamie a bugger, or some other foul language? Or had they really meant Jamie was a bastard, born without a father? If they did know he was illegitimate, how could they have discovered such a thing?

When Jamie had not returned for his evening meal, Emma felt panic rising. William began to feel more concerned than annoyed. Together they searched the loft in the house, the one above the stable and anywhere else they could think of.

'What if he is injured and out there alone?' Emma said, her voice trembling. 'Meg is sure he would not miss school just because of a fight. She says he's not afraid of any of them and he is top of his class for his work.'

'Perhaps I misjudged him,' William admitted. 'In my heart I've never believed he could be a coward.' Emma told him what Meg had said about the Mundy boys jeering and calling him a bastard.

'Oh my God! Surely they cannot have discovered our past? You go inside, Emma. I'll take the dogs and walk to the common to see whether the gypsies have seen him. He may have spent the day with Garridan. He always seems to be at ease with him, a bit like an elder cousin.' He stopped and stared down at her. 'His dog! I haven't seen Jill today, have you? He must have taken the wee collie with him.'

'No, I haven't seen her. She wasn't there when I fed Ben and Mel. It will soon be dark.'

William saw several gypsy children still playing outside the caravans. He asked where he could find Garridan.

'Garridan isn't here,' one of the older boys said. 'I find Fred for you?'

'Yes, please, laddie, you do that.' Fred came out of one of the brightly painted caravans further across the circle.

'I'm looking for Jamie. We thought he might have spent the day with Garridan. Do you know when he will be back?'

'He come back in two, maybe three weeks,' Fred said, suitably discreet as Garridan had asked. The gypsies were nothing if not loyal to their own kind.

'Has he taken his caravan? Could Jamie have gone with Garridan?'

'Garridan take his wife and the bambino.' Fred grinned, his fine white teeth gleaming in his weathered face. 'No place for Jamie to sleep then.'

'I see.' William felt despondent. What if Emma was right? What if he was lying injured somewhere? It was dark now.

'Have you seen Jamie on the common with his dog today, Fred?' The young gypsy man shook his head. He would not tell lies to Mr Sinclair but it was true he did not see the boy on the common today. He did not say Garridan could not have travelled many miles to the north yet, or that he had taken the little dog with him. Garridan had begun packing up as soon as he came back from riding his horse. He and his family had left soon after midday. Fred did not mention that Jamie and the dog had come to the camp very early this morning.

William set off home with the two collies at his heels, his eyes scanning the shadows in the fields and hedgerows as well as he could. He was sure Ben and Mel would run to Jamie if they heard him or picked up his scent.

Emma burst into tears when she saw William return alone and with no word of Jamie. She had been so sure he must have spent the day with the gypsies and they would have shared their meal, probably a rabbit stew.

'There's no more we can do tonight Emmie,' William said wearily. 'We must get some rest until daylight. Tomorrow we shall all search for him.' But Emma could not be comforted, even when they went to bed. They tossed and turned, unable to sleep. William took her in his arms and loved her tenderly but eventually they sought comfort in their earlier passionate loving, more ardent than either of them had been since the death of their last baby, almost a year ago. Their mutual ecstasy and satisfaction sent them to sleep with exhaustion, as it usually did, but it was a restless, troubled sleep and they wakened unrefreshed. They were both up and dressed before it was light. The cows still had to be milked, animals, workers and children had to be fed but Emma could not concentrate. Supposing Jamie had been injured? She shuddered and offered a silent prayer, 'Please God let him be alive and safe'. They all tried to act normally for the sake of the younger children but Meg sensed their anxiety and pleaded to be allowed to stay home from school.

'I must get the milk to the station in time for the train and pick up the empty churns,' William said, his own face showing lines of strain. 'I shall be back before you need to set off for school. If I meet anybody I will enquire if they have seen Jamie. If I have no news you can take Allan and John to school, Meg. See if you can learn anything of Jamie's whereabouts, then come back here and tell us if there is any news, anything at all. Someone must have seen him,' he said with a note of desperation. 'As soon as I get back from the station Tom and Cliff and I will search the common in case he caught his foot in a rabbit hole and sprained his ankle, or — or worse, got caught in a trap . . .' Immediately he wished he had kept that thought to himself when he heard Emmie stifle a sob.

'Polly will look after Marie and Janet and Peter. I must help you search,' Emma insisted. 'I can't stay in the house, I c-can't . . .'

'Maybe we could ask Billy if he has seen or heard anything?' Polly said, her cheeks growing pink. They all knew that the grocer's son and Polly often walked out together on her Sunday afternoon off, and occasionally he came and took her to a Saturday dance, but she rarely mentioned him in the house. 'He goes round the next two villages and most of the farms with deliveries. Maybe he has seen Jamie?' she suggested earnestly.

'I will write a note,' Emma said, 'and Meg can take it to Mr Nicholson at his shop after she has seen the boys into school. I would let you go yourself, Polly, but I need you so badly here. We c-can't leave the wee ones and I must get out there to search the sheds and lofts again.'

William was turning the milk cart onto the road to Silverbeck station when he saw the boy coming from the village. He was hailing him and waving a yellow envelope. He was already late with the milk but the boy was delivering a telegram and that was a rare occurrence. His heart thumped. He reached down and took it. 'Wait a minute laddie, while I see what it says.' Hastily he opened the envelope and read the brief message Bert Sinclair had sent. '*Jamie arrived here safely*'. He wiped his brow and breathed a sigh of relief.

'Thank God,' he muttered. 'Will you take this straight to Moorend laddie? Please? Mrs Sinclair will bless you for it. Tell her you met me on the road and I have seen it and I said you deserve an extra breakfast for delivering it all the way. I know she will agree.' The lad looked lean and hungry and the relief he brought with the telegram was immense. Emma would probably hug him in her joy. The boy's mouth watered in anticipation. He had not had anything to eat since yesterday afternoon.

All the way to the station and home again William's mind was asking silent questions. Why had Jamie run away from home? Why had he not confided in anyone? How had he got the fare for the train? Whatever had possessed him to go all the way to Scotland? He must have taken Jill with him. Surely he and Emma's father had not been in contact? Emma would have noticed if Jamie received a letter. Would her father send a letter as well as the telegram? Maybe he would see that Jamie wrote. Did Maggie know? All the way home his mood alternated between relief, bewilderment, and then anger that Jamie had caused so much worry.

Emma's first reaction had been intense relief to know that Jamie was safe and well. She fed the telegraph boy the biggest breakfast he had ever had in his life. Later, when she had time to consider, she felt a little hurt that Jamie had not confided in her and she wondered why he had gone all the way to Scotland. She didn't know how he had got the money for his train ticket and her only thought was to send him enough to return home.

As soon as he could speak to Emma alone, all William's thoughts and questions came tumbling out, mixed with his relief and anger at the anxiety he had caused them.

'Could he have been in contact with your father? Would he encourage him to go back to Scotland? The gossips will be every bit as bad there . . .'

'William! How can you think that? My father is an old man, but he is a wise one. He would never encourage Jamie to run away from home without telling us. What I want to know is how he got the money to buy his train ticket. He has not taken any money from my egg tin.'

'I don't know how he got his ticket,' William snapped irritably. 'The rumours will be spreading all over the village by now. They always grow with the repeating.' The atmosphere was strained. All Emma wanted was to have Jamie safely home again. William was plagued with thoughts that one or other of their families had encouraged his son to run away to Scotland rather than face malicious gossip. He had quite forgotten that he had done his best to avoid any gossip when he and Emma first settled at Moorend. He had led people to believe they were already married from the time he arrived in Yorkshire.

When letters arrived from both Bert Greig and Maggie, they did nothing to ease the tension. In fact, it grew when they read Maggie's letter claiming that Jamie had sensed for a long time that he was different because his father was more stern with him than with his brothers and sisters. After listening to the Mundy boys he thought William Sinclair was not his real father so that must be the reason he didn't love him the same as the others. He had decided it was better to run away since he was the cause of trouble and gossip.

I can understand his uncertainty would be made worse when he remembered his own grandmother called him a bastard. She told him he was not a Sinclair. I believe this has made it all too easy for Jamie to believe those horrid boys. They said his mother was a whore and he couldn't know who his father was. I didn't want to write such dreadful things but Joe thinks you should both know the truth and the malice which has driven Jamie away from home. He is not a coward. He is not afraid of physical punishment but he is only thirteen and he needs love and reassurance and understanding. Joe and I may not be parents but we can both understand how he must feel and none of the trouble is his fault.

It was a great surprise when he turned up here and we discovered he had run away from home. We had no idea there was any trouble from Emma's letters. Jim would be more than happy to keep him at Bonnybrae now that he is here. There is plenty of work for a boy. The lambing has begun and Father is not at all well. They are both pleased to keep him here if he wants to stay.

There was a little more asking about the rest of the family and telling Emma not to worry because they would all look after Jamie and see that he came to no harm. She said he had already made friends with Sir Reginald Capel's granddaughter who had become a pleasant and frequent visitor at Braeside, mainly because she has no local friends of her own age while she is home from boarding school.

Bert Greig's letter was short and a little stilted. He didn't go into detail but he said he had done his best to reassure Jamie that they both loved him and there was no doubt he was William's son because he was the image of him.

William was furious with his son and with his relatives for encouraging him to stay, while Emma had expected Jamie to come home again at once and return to school. Over the years they had often had discussions about work and family or life in general. As she matured, Emma had developed a mind of her own and William had learned to respect her intelligence and her lively sense of humour. They did not always agree, but they appreciated and accepted the other's point of view. Jamie was their eldest son; this time matters took a more serious turn and, for the first time in their lives, they quarrelled bitterly.

CHAPTER THIRTEEN

Rina Capel had visited Braeside almost every day during her school Christmas holidays, usually saying she wanted to see how the piglets were growing. The sow grew used to her appearing and soon saw that her piglets were in no danger when Rina sat in the straw beside her to cuddle one or other of them. Her favourite was the smallest of the litter and Rina named her Tiny Toes. She made Joe promise he would keep her for a mother pig and not make her into bacon when she grew big.

When she arrived home from school for the Easter holidays, Rina called at Braeside at the first opportunity. Maggie thought she would have forgotten them by now so she was touched and pleased to see her again. Fortunately, she had a fresh tray of toffee cooling.

Mr Capel the Younger had put every possible obstacle in their path when they were rebuilding Braeside but fortunately Sir Reginald had made sure that all the legal documents were in order and the lawyer had told Joe to refer any problems straight to him. Once he discovered there was nothing he could do they had not seen or heard from Rina's father again, but they knew he was not their friend.

'Do your parents know you have come to see us?' Maggie asked on that first visit of the Easter break from school.

'Grandfather knows I'm here. He says he missed my daily reports on the piglets when I went back to school.'

'I see, well, so long as your parents are not worrying . . .'

'They don't worry about me. I don't think they care where I ride so long as I don't pester them. Nat, my brother, has gone to stay with a school friend for most of the holidays. They're going sailing.'

'Nat? I thought your brother's name was Jonathan?'

'It is, but his school friends call him Nathan and now he says most of them call him Nat. It's easier to shout when they're playing cricket. So I call him Nat now. Mama gets very cross.'

'The piglets had to move away when they were weaned so they have gone up to the farm,' Maggie said, thinking it safer to change the subject back to pigs. 'My brother looks after them now.'

'Oh — but Tiny Toes! Mr Greig promised . . .' Maggie thought the tough wee Rina was going to burst into tears.

'Of course he did, and he never forgets a promise.' In fact it was clear that Rina had won Joe's heart as well as her own. 'We still have Tiny Toes, although she is getting quite big. She's in the spare sty. I have something else you might like to see?'

'Ooo what can it be?'

'Our first chicks hatched three days ago. Would you like to come with me to feed their mother, then they will come out from under her feathers?' It was clear to Maggie that Rina loved all living things and she was not afraid of getting dirty and helping to care for them. She suspected Rina's parents would probably blame her for encouraging the child but they enjoyed each other's company. Maggie had even agreed to teach her how to cook. She had not intended to do this but when it turned cold and wet during the Christmas holidays, Rina had still come to Braeside each day so she often joined Maggie in the kitchen, asking questions about what she was making and how to do it, and eventually progressing to, 'Can I have a go?'

'Mama doesn't let me go near the kitchens,' she confided, 'but I like to know how things are made.'

'Well you're just a wee girl, Rina. I expect she wants you to enjoy yourself.'

'I'm nearly eleven. Will you teach me how to make toffee? Please? And shortbread? Grandfather loves shortbread. He would let me make it in his kitchen and Mrs Mac never minds when I go there.'

The afternoon that Rina rode up to Braeside with Jamie mounted behind her was the biggest shock but the child didn't seem to realize anything could be wrong as she chattered on, explaining how she had seen old Mr Greig and Jamie on the road and offered him a ride. She guessed from the pleading look in Jamie's eyes that something was not quite right so instead of asking questions in front of Rina, she seized him in her arms and hugged him warmly. She sat them at her kitchen table and made a cup of tea with scones and gingerbread. Rina chattered as usual. Jamie answered when he had to and smiled at her, clearly as captured as herself and Joe by the child's innocence and natural curiosity. Eventually she said, 'I left Duke tethered to the gate post so I ought to go now but I'm very glad you have come for your holidays, Jamie. I'll ride over and see you tomorrow.'

After she had gone, Maggie listened in silent dismay as she learned the gist of the story behind Jamie's unexpected arrival. He had not intended to tell her the details about the Mundy brothers' nasty names and suggestions but somehow Maggie was so easy to talk to, it all poured out. Later he walked with her up to Bonnybrae to see Jim and her father. Their welcome was as warm as her own had been. Jim said he would be glad of a healthy young laddie to help him with the sheep.

'B-but I would like to stay here,' Jamie said urgently. 'All the time, I mean. I want to work and help you and earn my keep.' His grandfather raised his eyebrows but neither Jim nor Jamie noticed until he spoke.

'Ye'll have to understand then laddie, if ye really want to bide here and earn your living even after the Easter holidays are finished, you will have to learn to do every job there is to do, and that includes milking the cows.' His tone was grave.

'I do understand, Grandfather. I can milk you know, but I'm not as fast as Mam and Meg so Dad gets impatient. I don't mind doing it some of the time so long as I can do other things as well, like tend the sheep and work with the horses.'

'If ye're as good with the dogs as your mother says in her letters, ye can train our young bitch,' Jim said. For a moment Jamie was reminded of Jill and his eyes welled with tears. He turned sharply away, hoping they had not noticed. 'What's her name?' he asked gruffly. Jim whistled for the collie.

'Her name is Nell, nice and short, easy to call.' Jamie bent and fondled the young dog's ears. She was black and tan with a lovely white bib and she wagged her tail vigorously in welcome.

'I'll leave you with Jim to have a look round the few ewes which have already lambed,' Maggie said, 'then you can run down to Braeside. Joe will be home from work by then and I shall have a meal ready.'

'Thanks, Aunt Maggie,' Jamie said gratefully. It was such a relief that everyone seemed to accept his arrival and so far no one had blamed him or been angry.

As soon as he had eaten his meal Jamie went to bed. He was deadly tired and he wanted to be up early and at Bonnybrae the following morning. He was desperate to prove he had not run away because he was a slacker. He was not afraid of work. Maggie was relieved when he had gone to bed so that she could discuss things with Joe.

'The first thing I must do is write to Emmie and William and let them know he is here and safe, and why he has run away. He said he could not tell them the horrible things those boys had said about his parents, or the names they called him, but worst of all is he believes they may be speaking the truth.' Joe was silent for a while.

'Perhaps it would have been better for Emma and William to tell him about the past and the way things were, but he's just a boy yet. He would never understand. My father and your mother are a lot to blame. If Emma had not been sent away in such a rush to avoid all the bloody gossip-mongers . . .' Maggie put a soothing hand on his arm and smiled her understanding. Joe rarely swore or got angry.

'My own mother was even more to blame. William admitted the baby was his as soon as he knew Emma was expecting. He wanted to see her. He wanted to marry her straight away, but being banished to Yorkshire meant he had no job and not even a roof to offer a wife. I know they have had to work terribly hard but everything seemed to have worked out so well for them — until now.'

'Aye, well when you write let them know they should have seen the laddie was troubled and given him more reassurance. It is up to them to tell him about the circumstances of his birth. Even if he doesn't understand yet he will one day when he gets older and learns about love and temptation.'

'I do hope so,' Maggie said fervently, 'but William can be so stubborn, and I remember how short tempered he could be sometimes, though he never seemed to get impatient with Emmie, even when she first arrived at Bonnybrae and she was so nervous.'

'Maggie, if Jamie wanted to stay here,' Joe said slowly, 'permanently I mean, make his home with us, I wouldn't mind if you would like to have him. I've often thought what a good mother you would have made. I can understand why young Rina wants to come here so often.' Maggie smiled and stroked his lean face.

'It would be good to have someone young around but it will have to be Jamie's decision and I would never go against Emmie and William's wishes. As for Rina I suspect she will be in trouble if her father finds out where she exercises Duke, no doubt he will blame us for encouraging her. Thank goodness he has no authority to put us out of our home.'

'Don't worry about it, Maggie my love. You're only being your usual warm, welcoming self and the bairn obviously craves for company, even from old fogies like us,' Joe grinned.

Emma read, and re-read, the letters from Maggie and her father.

'It's clear they blame us for Jamie feeling uncertain about who he is. I can't believe he doesn't think you're his father. He's so like you in looks and he has inherited your patience and skill with training the collie dogs.'

'He's using all this as an excuse to get away from home now that he's ready to leave school and do some work!' William said angrily. 'Surely you can't believe all these stories?'

'I think you will believe them too if people like Thora Wilkins start spreading malicious rumours,' Emma said sharply. 'If she's heard she will probably make some remark when she sees us in church on Sunday. In fact I don't think I shall go until Jamie comes back home.' Polly heard them arguing and chewed her lip. Billy Nicholson had already heard some of the gossip in his father's grocery shop and he had said it was just the sort of thing a nasty woman like Mrs Wilkins would relish.

'You can't stay away just because our stupid son has taken it into his head he wants to run away,' William said angrily. 'That would make things worse.' Emma's soft mouth set and William guessed she was not going to be easily persuaded to face people until their son returned. 'Damn Jamie!' he muttered.

'That's the trouble with you!' Emma was unaware she had raised her voice. 'You do shout at him. You are impatient if he takes a bit longer to finish milking, but at least he makes a thorough job and you never give him credit for that. You expect him to do all sorts of things because he's the eldest. You're always telling him so.'

'You've never mentioned all this before.'

'I assumed you knew best what was good for a boy but I didn't realize what effect your criticism was having on him. Anyway he would never have taken any notice of the things the Mundy boy said if your mother hadn't called him a bastard and told him he was not a Sinclair. No wonder he isna sure who he is, or where he belongs.'

'That's ridiculous. You can't blame my mother. She was an old woman. She didna know what she was saying.'

'Oh she would know all right!' Emma rarely lost her temper but she was more upset than William realized. 'Your mother always meant what she said.' She heard Polly going to hang the washing out and realized she had probably overheard. Belatedly she lowered her voice but she almost spat the words through her teeth. 'She wanted to prevent you ever marrying me. That's why she insisted your father send you down here out of the way. She never came to our wedding. She never wished us well, or sent a present. She — she cast her venom at an innocent bairn. We thought Jamie was too young to take any notice, or remember. We were wrong.'

'Well, he needs to toughen up then and be a man!' William retorted.

'A man! He's a thirteen-year-old schoolboy for goodness' sake.'

'Old enough to travel to Scotland and leave school, it seems. Have you found out where he got the train fare yet? Are you sure he didn't take it from your egg money and you're covering up for him?' Emma's face went white with distress and William wanted to recall his words and take her in his arms and say he was sorry, but she turned abruptly away so he would not see her tears.

'I don't tell lies,' she snapped. 'You have always thought the worst of Jamie. You never did love him when he was a baby like you have loved the rest of them. Even when he was tiny and in a strange place, amongst strange people, you were irritated with him when he cried or needed to be fed.' William scowled. It was true he had never appreciated what a miracle it was to produce a child until Meg was born. She was only a few hours old when she curled her tiny fingers around one of his and looked up at him. He had not seen Jamie at that stage. Deep down he acknowledged he had been ridiculously jealous when he watched him snuggling into Emma's breasts and suckling eagerly. He had resented his own son,

God forgive him. Yet he could not let things rest. He was not the only one to blame.

'If you'd had to choose between Jamie and marrying me, you would have chosen him.' He hadn't meant to speak the words out loud, or so bitterly, but he had thought of this sometimes over the years, how he had had to wait for Emma's reply to his letter asking her to marry him. He knew Emma had grown to love him as he loved her but words spoken in anger could not be recalled.

That night when they went to bed Emma turned her back on her husband for the first time since they had been married. William was tempted to turn her over and make love to her whether she wanted it or not, but that would not be love and Emma would never forgive him. He grunted and turned on his side but it was a long time before either of them slept.

Emma wrote a letter to Jamie pleading with him to return home. She sent him a postal order to cash and pay for his train ticket. William was a good letter writer when he put his mind to it but it did not occur to him to write to his son and add his own pleas or reassurances.

During the Easter holidays, William was checking some of his in-calf heifers in one of the fields when he met a man out walking a small dog. The man leaned on the gate as though resting. He looked vaguely familiar, though William didn't think they had met. Later he realized the man had intended to waylay him.

'Good day to you, Mr Sinclair. It's very pleasant up here on a day like today,' he said. 'We don't often walk in this direction.'

'Good day to you.'

'You may not remember me. I am Edwin Thorpe. I teach your children at Silverbeck school.'

'Ah yes. I thought your face was familiar.' William smiled and held out his hand, wondering why the man wanted to talk to him.

'I was sorry to hear your son, Jamie, has gone to Scotland. I would like you to tell him if he returns when school opens again after the Easter holidays there will be no repercussions for him absenting himself ten days too early.'

'Mmm.' William's tone was grim. 'My son seems to think he is ready to leave school and start work. He wants to work with sheep.'

'I shall be sorry if he does not return for his last term to gain his leaving certificate. He is also in line for at least two of the special prizes in nature study and mathematics. Jamie is no coward; I know that. It was more than fighting which has driven him away and I feel partly responsible for any trouble in the school, though I must confess I had no idea of the malice and jealousy triggered by George Mundy and his brother. Mr Mundy has taken both his sons away from the school. They are to attend a boarding school in North Yorkshire, much to their mother's distress.'

'It is good of you to explain things, Mr Thorpe. Unfortunately I think Jamie has made up his mind not to return to school.'

'I am sorry to hear that. Whatever the truth of the matter I fear it seems the damage has been done as far as Jamie is concerned. Gossip is like the down from a plucked goose; it flies with the wind and there is no stopping it.'

William had no idea that the rumours about his family's affairs could have reached the schoolmaster's ears. He hadn't really believed Emma when she claimed stories would spread. Jamie running away had probably made things worse.

'I shall pass on your advice to Jamie to return but I cannot promise that he will be happy to do so.'

'Whatever the truth, it is nobody's business. It has always been clear to Miss Edgar and to myself that the Sinclair children come from a loving family. They are disciplined and well cared for. It is not always the wealthiest parents who care best for their children. Whatever Jamie decides, please tell him I wish him well for the future.'

'Thank you, Mr Thorpe, I shall do that. I appreciate you taking time to come and talk to me.' Mr Thorpe nodded briskly.

'It was a pleasure. Good day to you, Mr Sinclair.'

William walked on to the next field to count the young cattle but he frowned as he went. He hadn't really believed there was gossip flying around the village. He had thought it was the Mundy lads making schoolboy mischief. The painful thing was that Jamie had heard the gossip from them and believed it. In his heart William knew Emma was right, his mother was a lot to blame for sowing seeds of doubt in Jamie's young mind. He would not admit that, of course. There was still tension between them and a coolness William would never have believed possible with Emma. They spoke only if necessary. William had never seen this side of his wife before and he hated it. He knew Emma was miserable too and because he was missing Jamie it made things worse. He longed for the return of her cheery smile and her humour, and he was surprised to find he was missing her views when he wanted to discuss the farm and their work, the cows, their yields; in fact, the whole minutiae of everyday life.

Jamie could not believe how happy he felt during his first few days working at Bonnybrae and living with Uncle Joe and Aunt Maggie. On his first day it had been a surprise to see Rina again. She came riding up on her pony as he and Uncle Jim left the house after their midday meal to start another round of the in-lamb ewes in the two sheltered paddocks near the house. She slid lightly from her horse.

'Hello, Jamie. Mrs Grieg said you were working for your uncle so I've come to help.' She turned to Jim, giving him her wide beguiling smile. 'Do you mind if I take the bridle off Duke and let him graze a little somewhere? I would love to see the lambs, and maybe you would let me feed them, or something. Please Mr Sinclair?'

'You two know each other?' Jim said, staring at the two young faces.

'Rina gave me a lift on her horse when I arrived yesterday,' Jamie said.

'And I love animals,' Rina added. 'I would like to see how Mr Greig's piglets are growing, if I may?'

'All right,' Jim said, bemused. 'We have a pair of orphan lambs. You remember where they are, Jamie, in the wee pen next to the stable. Can you remember how to warm the milk to blood heat? Then you can feed one each.'

'Oh goody,' Rina said, clapping her hands.

'Where do you live, Rina?' Jim asked curiously. He thought he knew the children of most of the tenants round about, although sometimes they grew so fast he didn't recognize them.

'Over in that direction,' Rina waved vaguely towards the glen, east from Bonnybrae. It could be any one of three tenants, but Jim was busy and just nodded.

'You can come to the paddock, Jamie, when you have fed the lambs. I expect there will be one or two ewes lambing and we may need to bring them in for a night if this cold wind keeps up.' He eyed Rina's baggy breeches and thick jumper, which also looked two sizes too big for her. He turned away and hid a smile. She seemed a pleasant bairn whoever she was.

It was a busy afternoon with several ewes lambing. Two ewes needed help and had to be brought inside so Jim was glad of their help in guiding the stubborn sheep in the right direction, especially the one that already had a lamb and seemed unable to get the second one born. Jamie and Rina watched intently and neither of them seemed the least perturbed at the sight of blood and mucus when he withdrew his arm after feeling for the position of the lamb.

'It's as I thought. One of the legs was doubled back,' he told Jamie. 'I've straightened it out so she should lamb all right by herself now. I'm going in to wash my hands and have a cup of tea before we start milking. I'd like you to take Nell and check the gimmers in the top field, Jamie. Count them and make sure none of them look sickly or as though they might lamb. They're not due for three weeks yet but there's usually an odd one that lambs early for one reason or another.'

'Can I go with Jamie, Mr Sinclair?' Jim turned to look at the elfin face and wide blue eyes. There was something so innocent and genuine about the child, she was hard to resist.

'What about your parents? Will they wonder where you are?' he asked.

'Oh, Grandfather knows so it will be all right.'

'In that case, you had better both come into the house and have some tea. Maggie brought fresh scones up and we have raspberry jam. Will that do?'

'Mmm, it sounds delicious, doesn't it Jamie?' The child gave him her wide, enchanting smile showing square, even teeth.

'Hello Grandfather, I've just seen Uncle Jim helping a ewe to have her lamb,' Jamie said eagerly. James Sinclair shoved the kettle further on to the fire to boil. He liked a nap after his midday meal these days so he was glad the laddie had come and was so eager to work.

'You'll be ready for some tea now then. Wash your hands and set out the plates, will ye? Maggie goes home to her own house after dinner so we make our own tea. Mrs Edgar comes in after milking to make our evening meal. I expect you'll miss your mother running after you and getting everything ready, eh?'

'Meg and me always help when we get home from school,' Jamie said, not wanting to be reminded of his mam just now. His grandfather straightened up stiffly and turned towards the table.

'Oh, and who is this young lady then? I didn't know we had a visitor.'

'This is Rina,' Jim said with a smile. 'She has come to help Jamie with his work, she says. Yesterday I had no helpers and today I have two. They both want something to eat then they're going up to the top field to check the gimmers. I think they should all be all right but Jamie is an observant laddie. He reminds me of William, even the way he handles young Nell. She's attached herself to his heel already.'

'That's good then. The two older dogs are grand for around the steading and paddocks but ye'll be glad of Nell for the hill.' They all seated themselves around the table. James Sinclair looked at Rina, wondering where he could have seen her before with her dark curls and big blue eyes. She had a sprinkling of freckles across her neat little nose already, although summer was not yet here.

'Rina is an unusual name,' he mused, as much to himself as everyone else.

'Her real name is Catherine, isn't it?' Jamie supplied. 'Auntie Maggie calls her Rina though.'

'Ah, so you're Maggie's young visitor? She said she had enjoyed your visits at Christmas. Is this ye back from school for Easter?' He looked at his son. 'I dinna think her parents will approve o' ye making their daughter into a shepherdess, Jim.' He was smiling but his eyes looked slightly anxious, Jim thought. He frowned, struggling to remember what Maggie had said.

'Ye're Sir Reginald Capel's granddaughter, lassie? Good God, ye'll get me hung for letting ye help with the sheep.' Rina's eyes filled with tears and Jim looked at her in consternation.

'Please, please let me come again, Mr Sinclair. My grandfather knows where I am and he knows about Jamie coming to work here and that I've come to help him. I love the lambs and the piglets — and — and I hate when I have to go back to school and leave Duke and Scruff, and poor Dolly.'

'Well, well. Dinna get upset lassie. Eat another scone and plenty of jam,' James Sinclair urged, surprised by her vehemence. 'Who are this Duke and . . . ?'

'Duke is my pony. I ride him every day when I'm home. Grandfather bought him for me at Christmas. Dolly was my old pony. I've had her for ever. I really love her best but Grandfather says she is too old and too small for me now. Daddy wanted to — to kill her but Grandfather has promised she can stay in his paddock and enjoy her retirement like him. He takes her a sweet and an apple every day.'

'And Scruff? Who is Scruff?' Jamie asked curiously.

'He's my dog, but he lives with Grandfather. Daddy says he's a mongrel but he's lovely and I love him.'

Jim bit his lip and looked across at his father. It wouldn't be easy to stop the bairn from coming once she's made up her mind. Already she and Jamie seemed to have become good friends.

Later that evening, when they were alone, Jim broached the subject of Miss Catherine Capel. 'She says she's coming back tomorrow to help Jamie do his work. I told her he would have to start milking cows tomorrow but she said she would watch and maybe someday I would teach her how to do it. Imagine! Her father will play merry hell if he hears she's been here and that I let her come back.'

'I expect he will, if he finds out. Don't ye think if he and his wife cared enough about the lassie they would know where she spends her time? Surely they want her to be with them when she's on holiday. She's a loveable brat.' James Sinclair smiled. 'She seems to confide in Sir Reginald. If he thinks she shouldna come, he'll stop her.'

Rina returned to Bonnybrae almost every afternoon of the Easter holidays and it was clear she told her grandfather what she did and the things she learned.

'At least she's not deceiving the old laird,' Jim said to his father. 'Maggie is right when she says her parents don't seem to care where she spends her time so long as she doesn't bother them.'

Jamie missed Rina's company more than he had expected when she had to return to school. He had seen the tears in her eyes before she jumped on Duke's back and he had hugged her awkwardly as he would have done Meg or little Marie. Instead of galloping off in a great rush as she usually did she turned the horse around and asked tentatively, 'If I write you a letter will you reply to me and tell me what all the animals are doing and everything you are learning and if you have trained Nell to be a good sheep dog? I heard your uncle telling Mrs Greig you are really good at it, just like your father. Please promise you will reply.'

'All right,' Jamie mumbled guiltily. Both Aunt Maggie and Uncle Joe had tried to persuade him to write to his mother and father and explain to them himself why he had run away, but he hadn't done so although his mother had written to him twice and enclosed a short letter from Meg.

The following morning there was another letter from his mother, this time enclosing a short letter from his father telling him about his talk with Mr Thorpe and that everything would be all right if he came home in the next two days, ready to return to school at the beginning of the new term. His father even said he was proud of him because Mr Thorpe said he had earned at least two special prizes. He chewed his lip and said nothing but he left the letter for Aunt Maggie to read. That evening she tried hard to persuade him to return home and finish his schooling.

'I don't want to go back to Silverbeck,' he said stubbornly, reminding her of William as he had been at that age. 'School was all right but I'm learning a lot more here from Uncle Jim and I really like it. It is what I want to do with my life.'

Maggie was troubled by Jamie's refusal to write to his parents and explain how he felt. She showed William's short letter to her father.

'Emma's letters to Joe and me have been less warm and friendly than usual,' she said unhappily. 'I'm afraid they think we're to blame for giving Jamie a home.'

'Well, you canna turn the laddie out or they certainly wouldn't forgive you. Is Bert coming to you for his Sunday dinner this week?'

'Yes, he will be. Why do you ask?'

'I'd like a talk with him. If he agrees with what I have to say we'll have a talk with Jamie. I don't think he will go back home for a while, not until he grows up and understands things better, but at least he might reply to Emma's letters.

She's bound to be hurt and she didn't deserve this kind o' trouble.'

At first, Bert Greig was reluctant to talk to Jamie about the past and the part they had both played in keeping William and Emma apart, even though it had not been intentional.

'A young laddie like Jamie canna understand the temptations of desire. He might blame his mother more than he does already.'

'He'll be more likely to blame his father if anybody,' James Sinclair replied wryly. 'But at least we can explain why his parents didn't marry before he was born and we were both responsible for that.'

'Maybe we were in a way,' Bert Greig admitted, 'but I'd never have sent Emma away if she had told us William was the father.'

'Aye well, what's done can't be undone and we did our best at the time, or at least you did. I did what pleased Mary but I should have known her mind was already becoming disturbed when she was so bitter and unhappy. I never really wanted to send William away.' The two old men talked for a while then had a short nap, as they usually did in the afternoons. Feeling more refreshed they agreed to tell their grandson the part they had played in the past and why he was born out of wedlock.

Jamie wondered whatever his grandfathers could want him for on a peaceful Sunday afternoon. He had been up the hill with Nell and he was pleased with the way the collie seemed to have taken to him and was beginning to obey all his commands, and almost anticipate what he wanted her to do.

'She's so intelligent,' he said to his Uncle Jim.

'Well, she is the same way bred as Queenie was, your father's bitch. You'll maybe not remember her?'

'Yes of course I do. Dad has a bitch out of her called Bess. When she had pups he — he gave me one of my own.' He gulped hard. He couldn't bear to think of Jill and the way he had left her behind. Jim could see something was upsetting him and he thought maybe the puppy had died. He changed the subject.

'Your grandfathers are both in the sitting room. They want to talk to you before we have our cup of tea and start the milking.' Jamie was convinced they would try to persuade him he must go home. His heart sank.

At first he was bewildered when they started telling him about his mother and father and how his mother had come to Bonnybrae as a young maid, how nervous she had been, then how she had learned to love the animals and how hard she worked.

'She was a bonny lassie too with her long, dark hair and those bright eyes like emeralds,' Grandfather Sinclair said. 'Ye'll not understand until ye're a bit older but your father was a young man and he liked her a lot. One day they went to the hill to gather the sheep. The mist came down so they had to spend the night on the hill until it lifted.' He cleared his throat awkwardly, uncertain how to go on.

'Och they were young and innocent the pair o' them,' Bert said brusquely. 'They should have resisted temptation but ye'll ken one day that it's easy to say that when a pretty lassie attracts ye. Anyway your mother ended up expecting a baby but she — well, she didn't know until you were well on the way, Jamie. We, your grandmother and me — well, we bothered too much about the gossips and what folks would say.' He flushed. 'We were ashamed o' her having a bairn without a husband and she wouldna tell us who your father was. I sent her away to ma brother and his wife near Glasgow so that the folks in Locheagle wouldn't know. I'm sorry now. I shall regret it to ma dying day, but I thought I was doing the best for everybody.'

'Ye were not the only one to blame, Bert,' James Sinclair assured him. 'We all had too much pride and bothered what other folks would say, especially Mary. As soon as William heard wee Emmie was expecting a bairn he knew it was his and he told us all. He wanted to see her and ask her to marry him, but she had already gone to Glasgow and he didna know where to find her. I shall never really understand what made his mother so bitter because she had always liked Emma. I agreed to send him off to Yorkshire to please her and I've regretted it ever since. Your grandmother hated gossip and she felt responsible for your mother — because she was her maid, she was supposed to be safe under our roof. I shouldna have listened to her, I know that now. Anyway your father was down in Yorkshire working for a living on one o' the farms, but he didn't have anywhere to live, for him or a wife.'

'That's right.' Bert nodded. 'He slept in a loft with two other men so Emmie couldna have gone with him, even if we had known he was your father.'

'As soon as he got the chance to rent a farm — the place he has now — he wrote to ask Emma to marry him. He promised to come up and take her back.'

'She was still at ma brother's,' Bert Greig said, shaking his head in sorrow. 'His wife was a lazy, spiteful woman. I should never have sent my poor bairn to stay with her. The poor lassie fell down the ladder while she was cleaning out the loft. It brought on the birth o' her bairn so you came a bit before your time, Jamie. That's why you were born before your parents could get married. But they did get married as soon as it could be arranged. We were all there in the kirk at Locheagle to see them, and you were christened by your Aunt Julie's father. Afterwards they took you all the way to Yorkshire on the train, you and William's dog, Queenie.'

'That's all there is to it laddie,' James Sinclair said with a sigh. 'I don't know how those fellows got hold of the story but there's no doubt William is your father and Emma is a good wife and mother. Ye should be proud o' them, Jamie. They have worked hard to make a home for ye all. Dinna be like us laddie and pay attention to the gossips in this world. We both rue the part we played for the sake o' respectability, don't we Bert?'

'Aye we do indeed,' Bert agreed sorrowfully, 'and your Grandmother Greig rued it most of all because her only daughter was so far away.'

'I knew there was a secret!' Jamie burst out. 'So if my father really is my own father, why didn't they explain?'

'William certainly is your father, laddie, there's no doubt about that. Ye're the image o' him. Ye even like your own way and want to make your own decisions the way he did,' James Sinclair said with a wry smile. 'Ye have his gift with the dogs.'

'But Cyril Mundy still said I'm a bastard!'

'That's a nasty word, laddie. Try to forget it,' Bert advised gently. 'Ye're a fine laddie and ye have a mother and father who love ye. They have tried to do what they think is best for ye.'

'But why couldn't they have told me?' Jamie demanded. As far as he could see it was all a lot of fuss about the date his parents got married, and it had nothing to do with not knowing who his father was and whether or not it was some stranger. He looked from one grandfather to the other, then he said slowly, 'I really like living up here and I'm not bothered about going back to school. If I promise to write them a letter, can I stay here? I promise to work hard.' He looked pleadingly at the old men, unaware they were giving an inner sigh of relief.

'Well, if James is willing to keep ye here,' Bert said thoughtfully, 'I think the least ye can do is write a letter every week. I remember how much your grandmother looked forward to getting your mother's letters and hearing how you were getting on and what they were doing on the farm.'

'We would all like to keep ye here, laddie,' James Sinclair said, 'but I don't think your mother and father will be very pleased with us for keeping ye. They might be more likely to agree if you promise to go back to Yorkshire twice every year to see them. At least they will know they'll see ye again.' He held up his hand when Jamie would have protested. 'I'll pay your train fare. Ye needna worry about that, but we must have your parents' agreement. In fact, I will write to them myself. It's only fair, and it might help.'

Jamie felt as though a huge weight had been lifted from him. He knew who he was and where he belonged and now he had two families who loved him. He thought about Rina.

She loved her grandfather but she didn't seem very sure that her parents even wanted her in her own home, so he was not the only one with uncertainties. He remembered he had promised to answer the letters if she wrote to him. He had thought she would forget, or wouldn't be bothered, when she returned to her friends at school, but already he had received a letter and she had only been back a week.

On Sunday evening, he sat at the kitchen table with the writing paper Aunt Maggie had bought for him and arranged his pen and bottle of black ink. He wrote to Rina first because it was easy to tell her the news of all the animals and answer her questions. Then he chewed the end of his pen, deep in thought. Eventually he wrote to his parents telling them he was sorry if he had worried or upset them, and how his grandfathers had explained about the past.

So even if I am a bastard, like Cyril Mundy said, at least I know my father really is my father, and I always knew Mam was not what they called her.

I don't want to return and go back to school. I shall be fourteen soon and I'm enjoying working with the sheep with Uncle Jim. Even the milking doesn't seem so bad. There is a lad in the bothy who is fifteen but he is not as big as I am and he's even slower at milking than I am. I think we shall be good friends if I can stay here. Grandfather Sinclair says he will pay my train fare so that I can come home to see you all twice a year. I am staying with Aunt Maggie and Uncle Joe and I expect you would say Aunt Maggie is spoiling me but she is as strict as Mam about some things, like clean clothes and good manners and she says I must write to you every week — but I will do that anyway if you give me permission to stay and learn to be a proper shepherd. Uncle Jim says Nell, the wee collie, works better for me already than she does for him, but I miss Jill terribly and I hope she is happy with Garridan. He promised to take care of her and not to sell her to anyone else.

He had to stop writing to blink away the tears when he thought of Jill. Eventually he finished the letter and put it in the envelope, ready for Uncle Joe to post when he went to work on Monday morning.

'There's three letters for you, Mrs Sinclair,' Polly announced with a smile. She had met the postman in the yard and she recognized Jamie's handwriting on one. She hoped fervently that it would cheer up her mistress and lighten the atmosphere in the household. She had never known Mr and Mrs Sinclair to be so silent with each other before. Her Aunt Ivy said it would all blow over once the gossip died down.

Usually William waited until the end of the day to read letters from the family to enjoy them at leisure but he waited for Emmie to tear open the letter from Jamie and stood behind her chair, one hand warm and firm on her shoulder as they read the letter together. She gasped softly when she read about hers and William's fathers explaining everything. When she got to the bit where Jamie said the main thing was that his father really was William, even if he was a bastard, as Cyril had said, she glanced up at her husband and saw the pain on his face. She put up a hand to cover his and squeezed it warmly. It was the first gesture of affection Emmie had shown since Jamie had run away. His face softened. He knew she held him partly responsible with his stern attitude towards his first born, and deep down he accepted he had always felt a stupid frisson of jealousy for the deep love and affection Emma and Jamie had always shared. But as she read on, Emma realized Jamie was not coming home. He was not returning to school. He wanted to live in Scotland. She pushed herself away from the table with a faint moan. Her head spun and for the first time in her life, Emma fainted. It was fortunate William was standing close enough to catch her before she fell to the floor.

'Emma! Oh, Emmie,' he gasped, staring down into her white face. He cradled her in his arms and made for the stairs. 'Polly! Send Thomas to get the doctor. Tell him to hurry.'

Polly dare not argue and in truth she had never seen her hardy little mistress faint before, even when she was expecting her babies. Thomas was in time to catch Doctor Dunhill setting out in his pony and trap to begin his rounds.

'Jump in, lad, and we'll go to Moorend right now. It's not often the Sinclairs need me. You say you don't know what happened to cause Mrs Sinclair to collapse?'

William laid Emma gently on the bed and when Polly showed the doctor upstairs he was kneeling beside her, wiping her pale face with a damp cloth and murmuring words of encouragement to please come back to him. He waited silently while the doctor examined Emma, ignoring her protests that she was fine now and she didn't know what had come over her.

'I think you are anaemic, Mrs Sinclair,' Doctor Dunhill said kindly, 'and there's little wonder after your last ordeal and losing your baby. Is it possible you could be starting another baby?'

'Oh no, Doctor! At least . . . I-I don't think so.' Emma looked up at William. His lips were parted; his eyes round with shock. They were both remembering how they had clung to each other for comfort the night they thought Jamie was lost, before they knew he had run away to Scotland.

'Mmm, it's too soon to tell, but I wouldn't be surprised. Whether you are or not you're needing to build yourself up.' Doctor Dunhill turned to William. 'You will need to see your wife takes more rest and eats plenty of good red meat and as much fresh liver as she can manage. Producing seven — or is it eight? — babies has taken its toll, even if there is not another on the way.'

When the doctor had gone, Emma sat up and swung her legs to the floor.

'No, no, Emmie.' William gently pushed her back against the pillows. 'Rest a while. I will bring you a fresh cup of tea with a tot of whisky. I'll bring up the other two letters as well. Who were they from, do you know?'

'I didn't open them but I know one is from Maggie and Joe. I think the other is from your father.' Emma sank into the pillows. She felt exhausted without knowing why. When William returned he set the letters on the bed beside her, then eased her into the crook of his arm and gave her the cup.

'There's more than a tot of whisky in this,' Emma said after the first sip.

'Drink it up. It will do you good. If I have given you another baby Emmie, I think we should ask Maisie Blackford if she will come every weekday.'

'I have never fainted before. It's too early to know about a baby yet. It — it was the shock. Jamie sounded so cheerful and so normal in the first part of his letter then — then he said he isn't coming home. Oh William! I can't bear it.' William waited until she had drunk all the tea. He felt the spirits might perk her up. He took the cup away then knelt beside her, taking her hand in his as he stroked her wrist.

'I am missing Jamie too, more than I ever thought possible considering he's still a schoolboy. Cliff misses him too. They got on well even though he is so young. But I'm glad our fathers explained and that he accepts what happened. I'm sure he knows we both love him.'

'He must know that . . .'

'If he had to run away I am thankful he went to folks he knows who will be kind to him and not take advantage of his youth.'

'Oh I'm sure Jim would never do that. He sounds so happy to be working with the sheep and the dogs. He must have sold Jill to Dan to get the money for his fare.'

'Yes, I've not seen Garridan lately but I'll take a walk up there and ask him. Meanwhile, Emmie,' he hesitated, then went on, 'I know you blame me for Jamie running away and . . .'

'No, no I don't, not anymore,' Emma insisted. 'I've heard some of the gossip myself and it would be worse for Jamie. He's so young to understand about life and those Mundy boys are cruel bullies. I blame them for driving him away and I'm glad Mr Thorpe refused to have them back at the school.'

'Emmie, I hate when we disagree,' William said softly. 'However much I shall miss my eldest son, you know I would miss you more, don't you?'

'I know that in my heart, William. It's just that I've felt so miserable without Jamie around.'

'It's only natural. Shall we see what my father and Maggie and Joe have to say?' He handed Emma the letters. They read them together.

'Maggie and Joe both seem to enjoy having Jamie to live with them. They would have made lovely parents,' Emma said. 'I'll bet they're spoiling him when he's the only one.'

'I can imagine Maggie making him some of her butterscotch toffee,' William grinned, 'but she'll make sure he washes behind his ears!' They both smiled.

'See here's my father's letter. He says they will not keep him at Bonnybrae if it is going to make a rift in our families again, especially when things were getting more normal. Then he goes on to say what a grand worker Jamie is with the sheep and the dogs. Jim thinks he will be as good with the horses as I am, in time. If we are willing to let him stay at Bonnybrae he and Jim would be proud to have him. He says it's good to have a youngster about the place again. He has not mentioned anything to Jamie about his future but he says we should consider it, especially as we have a brood of children and none of us know what the future holds. Jim has no sons to follow in his footsteps and he would welcome a nephew like Jamie to carry on at Bonnybrae.'

Emma looked up at him, her eyes swimming with tears as he folded the letter and returned it to the envelope. She saw the shadows in William's eyes too.

'It's so hard to give up a child,' she said.

'I know. I confess you were right about me being jealous of Jamie, Emmie. Before we were married I was sure if you had to choose between Jamie and me, you would choose him. Your letters were all full of him and you didn't even mention us getting married, even though I wrote twice to plead with you.' Emma reached out and stroked his cheek. He sounded so like a small boy who had grazed his knees and wanted them made better. She smiled tenderly.

'The thought of moving to Yorkshire, especially after staying with my uncle and aunt, appalled me. I admit it. It was so far away. But that was then. You must know how much I love you now, William. You will always come first and last with me now.'

'Oh, Emmie. You really mean that?' Emma held out her arms.

'Let me show you.'

THE END

THE JOFFE BOOKS STORY

We began in 2014 when Jasper agreed to publish his mum's much-rejected romance novel and it became a bestseller.

Since then we've grown into the largest independent publisher in the UK. We're extremely proud to publish some of the very best writers in the world, including Joy Ellis, Faith Martin, Caro Ramsay, Helen Forrester, Simon Brett and Robert Goddard. Everyone at Joffe Books loves reading and we never forget that it all begins with the magic of an author telling a story.

We are proud to publish talented first-time authors, as well as established writers whose books we love introducing to a new generation of readers.

We have been shortlisted for Independent Publisher of the Year at the British Book Awards three times, in 2020, 2021 and 2022, and for the Diversity and Inclusivity Award at the Independent Publishing Awards in 2022.

We built this company with your help, and we love to hear from you, so please email us about absolutely anything bookish at feedback@joffebooks.com

If you want to receive free books every Friday and hear about all our new releases, join our mailing list: www.joffebooks.com/contact

And when you tell your friends about us, just remember: it's pronounced Joffe as in coffee or toffee!

ALSO BY GWEN KIRKWOOD

THE MAXWELL FAMILY QUARTET
Book 1: AN ORPHAN OF SCOTLAND
Book 2: THE SECRETS THAT BIND US
Book 3: DREAMS OF THE VALLEY
Book 4: SOMEWHERE TO CALL HOME

THE SINCLAIR FAMILY SAGAS
Book 1: MOORLAND MIST
Book 2: MOOREND FARM
Book 3: RETURN TO BONNYBRAE
Book 4: A SCOTTISH DESTINY
Book 5: LOVE HAS NO BORDERS

Printed in Great Britain
by Amazon

28195584R00110